BOOTLEGGERS

By Whiskey Jack Peters

For information, please email teslabookstore@vivaldi.net.

First Edition published 2019

With special acknowledgement
to T.C. De Witt for his contributions
in the crafting of this novel.

"A father is a man who expects his son to be as good a man as he meant to be."
—Frank A. Clark

"Some call it bootlegging. Some call it racketeering. I call it a business."
—Al Capone

INTRODUCTION

In the United States, once the battle against slavery was won (indeed, even before it), social moralists turned to other issues, such as Mormon polygamy and the temperance movement. But the war that became most prominent was that on alcohol; a war that led to the National ban of alcohol. On November 18, 1918, prior to ratification of the Eighteenth Amendment, the U.S. Congress passed the temporary Wartime Prohibition Act, which banned the sale of alcoholic beverages having an alcohol content of greater than 1.28%. This Act, which had been intended to save grain for the war effort, was passed after the armistice ending World War I was signed on November 11, 1918. The Wartime Prohibition Act took effect June 30, 1919, with July 1, 1919 becoming known as the "Thirsty-First".

Prohibition in the United States was a nationwide constitutional ban on the production, importation, transportation, and sale of alcoholic beverages from 1920 to 1933. This ban extended to Canada in the same years. Most of the provinces enacted prohibition during that first World War, and opted to extend the ban on alcohol following the end of the war. Between 1878 and 1928 about 75% of Canadian breweries had closed. During the nineteenth century, alcoholism, family violence, and saloon-based political corruption prompted prohibitionists, led by pietistic Protestants, to end the alcoholic beverage trade in America and Canada, to cure the ill society, and weaken the political opposition. One result was that many communities in the late-nineteenth and early-twentieth centuries introduced alcohol prohibition, with the subsequent enforcement in law becoming a hotly debated issue. Prohibition supporters, called "drys", presented it as a victory for public morals and health.

Promoted by the "dry" crusaders, the movement was led by those pietistic Protestants and social Progressives in the Prohibition — Democratic, and Republican parties. It gained a national grassroots base through the Woman's Christian Temperance Union. After 1900, it was coordinated by the Anti-Saloon League. Opposition from the beer industry mobilized "wet" supporters from the Catholic and German Lutheran communities. They had funding to fight back, but by 1917–18 the German community had been marginalized by the nation's war against Germany, and the brewing industry was shut down in state after state by the legislatures and finally nationwide under the Eighteenth Amendment to the United States Constitution in 1920. Enabling legislation, known as the Volstead Act, set down the rules for enforcing the federal ban and defined the types of alcoholic beverages that were prohibited. For example, religious use of wine was allowed. Private ownership and consumption of alcohol were not made illegal under federal law, but local laws were stricter in many areas, with some states banning possession outright. As the push for stricter control and organized efforts to see the entire Nation dry both grew, so too did the wet opposition. Criminal gangs were able to gain control of the beer and liquor supply for many cities. The era of the BOOTLEGGER had begun.

As early as 1925, journalist H. L. Mencken believed that Prohibition was not working. "Prohibition worked best when directed at its primary target: the working-class poor." Historian Lizabeth Cohen writes: "A rich family could have a cellar-full of liquor and get by, it seemed, but if a poor family had one bottle of home-brew, there would be trouble." Working-class people were inflamed by the fact that their employers could dip into a private cache while they, the employees, could not.

Before the Eighteenth Amendment went into effect in January 1920, many of the upper classes stockpiled alcohol for legal home consumption after Prohibition began. They bought the inventories of liquor retailers and wholesalers, emptying out their warehouses, saloons, and club storerooms. President Woodrow Wilson moved his own supply of alcoholic beverages to his Washington residence after his term of office ended. His successor, Warren G. Harding, relocated his own large supply into the White House after inauguration.

After the Eighteenth Amendment became law, the United States embraced bootlegging. In just the first six months of 1920 alone, the federal government opened 7,291 cases for Volstead Act violations. In just the first complete fiscal year of 1921, the number of cases violating the Volstead Act jumped to

29,114 violations and would rise dramatically over the next thirteen years. Grape juice was not restricted by Prohibition, even though if it was allowed to sit for sixty days it would ferment and turn to wine with a twelve percent alcohol content. Many folks took advantage of this as grape juice output quadrupled during the Prohibition era.

Making alcohol at home was common among some families with wet sympathies during Prohibition. Stores sold grape concentrate with warning labels that listed the steps that should be avoided to prevent the juice from fermenting into wine. Some drug stores sold "medical wine" with around a 22% alcohol content. In order to justify the sale, the wine was given a medicinal taste. Home-distilled hard liquor was called bathtub gin in northern cities, and moonshine in rural areas of Virginia, Kentucky, North Carolina, South Carolina, Georgia, and Tennessee. Homebrewing good hard liquor was easier than brewing good beer. Since selling privately distilled alcohol was illegal and bypassed government taxation, law enforcement officers relentlessly pursued manufacturers. In response, bootleggers modified their cars and trucks by enhancing the engines and suspensions to make faster vehicles that, they presumed, would improve their chances of outrunning and escaping agents of the Bureau of Prohibition, commonly called "revenue agents" or "revenuers". These cars became known as "moonshine runners" or "'shine runners". Shops with wet sympathies were also known to participate in the underground liquor market, by loading their stocks with ingredients for liquors, including bénédictine, vermouth, scotch mash, and even ethyl alcohol, which anyone could purchase legally.

Mark H. Moore states that contrary to popular opinion, "violent crime did not increase dramatically during Prohibition" and that organized crime "existed before and after" Prohibition. Kenneth D. Rose, a professor of history at California State University-Chico, maintains that the idea of a "prohibition crime wave was rooted in the impressionistic rather than the factual."

Another source, however, opines that organized crime received a major boost from Prohibition. Mafia groups limited their activities to prostitution, gambling, and theft until 1920, when organized bootlegging emerged in response to Prohibition. A profitable, often violent, black market for alcohol flourished. Prohibition provided a financial basis for organized crime to flourish. In one study of more than 30 major U.S. cities during the Prohibition years of 1920 and 1921, the number of crimes increased by 24%. Additionally, theft and burglaries increased by 9%, homicides by 12.7%, assaults and battery rose by 13%, and drug addiction by 44.6%. Consequently, police department costs rose by 11.4%. This was largely the result of "black-market violence" and the diversion of law enforcement resources elsewhere. Despite the Prohibition movement's hope that outlawing alcohol would reduce crime, the reality was that the

Volstead Act led to higher crime rates than were experienced prior to Prohibition and the establishment of a black market dominated by criminal organizations. The Saint Valentine's Day Massacre produced seven deaths, considered one of the deadliest days of mob history. A 2016 NBER paper showed that South Carolina counties that enacted and enforced prohibition had homicide rates increase by about 30 to 60 percent relative to counties that did not enforce prohibition.

However, some scholars have attributed the crime during the Prohibition era to increased urbanization, rather than to the criminalization of alcohol use. In some cities, such as New York City, crime rates decreased during the Prohibition era. Crime rates overall declined from the period of 1849 to 1951, making crime during the Prohibition period less likely to be attributed to the criminalization of alcohol itself.

The historian Kenneth D. Rose corroborates historian John Burnham's assertion that during the 1920s "there is no firm evidence of this supposed upsurge in lawlessness" as "no statistics from this period dealing with crime are of any value whatsoever". Rose writes: "Opponents of prohibition were fond of claiming that the Great Experiment had created a gangster element that had unleashed a 'crime wave' on a hapless America." The WONPR's Mrs. Coffin Van Rensselaer, for instance, insisted in 1932 that "the alarming crime wave, which had been piling up to unprecedented height was a legacy of

Prohibition." But Prohibition can hardly be held responsible for inventing crime, and while supplying illegal liquor proved to be lucrative, it was only an additional source of income to the more traditional criminal activities of gambling, loan sharking, racketeering, and prostitution. The notion of the prohibition-induced crime wave, despite its popularity during the 1920s, cannot be substantiated with any accuracy, because of the inadequacy of records kept by local police departments.

In October 1930, just two weeks before the congressional midterm elections, bootlegger George Cassiday—"the man in the green hat"—came forward and told members of Congress how he had bootlegged for ten years. One of the few bootleggers ever to tell his story, Cassiday wrote five front-page articles for The Washington Post, in which he estimated that 80% of congressmen and senators drank. The Democrats in the North were mostly wets, and in the 1932 election, they made major gains. The wets argued that Prohibition was not stopping crime and was actually causing the creation of large-scale, well-funded, and well-armed criminal syndicates. As Prohibition became increasingly unpopular, especially in urban areas, its repeal was eagerly anticipated.

When Prohibition was repealed in 1933, many bootleggers and suppliers with wet sympathies simply moved into the legitimate liquor business. Some crime syndicates moved their efforts into expanding their protection rackets to cover legal liquor sales and other business areas.

By the late-1920s a new opposition mobilized nationwide. Wets attacked Prohibition as causing crime, lowering local revenues, and imposing "rural" Protestant religious values on "urban" United States. Prohibition ended with the ratification of the Twenty-first Amendment, which repealed the Eighteenth Amendment on December 5, 1933. Some states continued statewide prohibition, marking one of the last stages of the Progressive Era.

Research shows that Prohibition reduced overall alcohol consumption by half during the 1920s, and consumption remained below pre-Prohibition levels until the 1940s, suggesting that Prohibition did socialize a significant proportion of the population in temperate habits, at least temporarily. Rates of liver cirrhosis "fell by 50% early in Prohibition and recovered promptly after Repeal in 1933. Criticism remains that Prohibition led to unintended consequences such as a century of Prohibition-influenced legislation and the growth of urban crime organizations; though some scholars have argued that violent crime did not increase dramatically, while others have argued that crime during the Prohibition era was properly attributed to increased urbanization, rather than the criminalization of alcohol use. As an experiment it lost supporters every year, and lost tax revenue that governments needed when the Great Depression began in 1929.

CHAPTER ONE

Texada Island, British Columbia, Canada
13 November, 1920

The sun set over the swamplands of Texada Island, British Columbia painting the Canadian landscape in a golden glow, speckling the pine trees, and rippling over the blue waters. It was a peaceful, serene, unseasonably warm November day in the undisturbed wilderness. The steady rhythm of croaking frogs and buzzing cicadas who had yet to see fit to retreat into hibernation was broken by the sound of heavy footfalls through the watery mire.

Breaking through the treeline, the silhouette of a man appeared with a raggedy hunting dog at his side, both of them panting for breath; the dog panting from the unseasonable humidity, the man winded from his age. Abraham Calloway had grey at his temples and deep lines on his face; and yet, there was a youthful glimmer in his eye – puckish and roguish. He had a scruff of growth lining his once powerful jaw, now rounded from his five plus decades on the planet. Stopping to wipe his brow with a faded hanky that he pulled from his well-worn pants, he took a long draw of air and exhaled before stuffing the handkerchief back in his pocket, adjusting the large gunny sack over his shoulder, and continuing his tromp through the wetlands.

Abe was nimble and moved with a purpose. His unkempt hair stuck to his sweaty neck. His hands were powerful and muddy. The sunlight glinting off the stream of water to his left reflected into his eyes and caused him to squint, but he did not slow down. He clicked his tongue to keep his dog, Chip, close as he came to the edge of the trees and tall grass.

Peeking through the bullrush along the side of a steady river, Abe crouched. His eyes shifted warily among the reeds, looking for any sign of trouble, an odd action so far out in the middle of the wild. He squinted and scanned slowly every inch of the land before him. Minutes ticked by, his breathing steadied. A pair of Steller's jays took flight and swooped low overhead before flittering off towards the distant mountains. Chip's head lifted to watch them pass, but Abe's eyes remained focused. The sun began to move to the horizon, twilight approaching.

Finally satisfied, he patted his dog on the head and he rose from the bush. Side-by-side, the scraggly pair continued through the swamp. They splashed through the shin-deep water of the moving river and back into the trees hedging the adjacent bank. The sun attempted to follow, but the hanging branches were thick with leaves that created a canopy of shadows. Abe and Chip disappeared into the darkness. The sun finally dipped behind the trees and night began to crawl over Texada Island.

Some distance into the sunless forest, Abe entered a clearing facing a small house that was little more than a shack.

He did not slow, making a beeline for the small, simple wood structure in the heart of the swamp surrounded by thick foliage – his home.

He stomped his boots on the front porch. The damp, old wood protested the forceful action, but helped clean his feet from clumps of mud nonetheless. Chip scraped his paws on a pile of chopped firewood. Abe nodded in approval, and the pair entered the home.

Abe pushed his way through the creaking door as Chip slipped around his legs and hurried to a water dish waiting for him on the floor nearby. The old man slammed the door shut causing the collection of antlers on the walls to bounce. He bolted the locks, though the wood was so worn, it wouldn't take much force to kick the thing in, were one so inclined. The windows were dusty, yet Abe moved to the glass beside the front door and peered outside, back the way he came. His careful, sharp eyes took a final scan of the area before he drew the curtains over the grimy glass.

The shack was a small home; a cabin in the woods. Hunting and fishing gear, a small bed with worn out blankets where Chip had already made himself comfortable, a small table and two stools. A small radio was set on a shelf next to some dusty books that had probably never been read. The place had seen many winters of ice fishing and many summers of hunting.

Abe dropped the gunny sack to the floor beside the entrance and stretched his aching back with a long grunt. As the sack hit the floor, it opened, revealing a half dozen bags of corn. He bent and dragged the sack across the floor toward his small pantry in what one might call a kitchen. There was a water basin and along the wall was a small cast iron stove.

Picking up a lantern and using his thumb to ignite a matchstick, Abe lit the oil soaked wick and stepped to the far end of the shack and the rear door. He unbolted it and stepped outside into the shadowy backyard. As he did, he gave a quick whistle to Chip.

Behind the shack, through the thick trees and bushes, there was a small path that had been walked countless years. Stepping down the path surrounded by the growing night, Abe raised the lantern, and the glowing yellow-orange revealed a collection of metal and wood purposefully situated in the trees. It was a handmade whiskey still set up near the creek in the woods behind Abe's home. He grinned, the crows feet more defined by it, and yet, conversely, the youthful mischief even more clear. Abraham Calloway was a moonshiner - a bootlegger.

He didn't take his eyes off the still, but he spoke in a baritone rumble that was his smoky voice, "Time to get to work, old friend." He could have been speaking to Chip or the still itself. He stepped forward and lit a fire beneath the big pot.

Abe put his hands on a large glass keg of sugar molasses-water solution and opened the container. The keg was marked the 5th of December, 1919. Chip slipped around his master and sniffed the lid. Abe dipped a wooden spoon into the keg, brought it up, and stuck his tongue on the end, tasting it. He flinched at the strong flavor but grinned, happy with the stinging results. Chip sniffed at the spoon.

"Easy, boy," Abe grunted, "You know better. This stuff is way too strong for you."

Abe scratched the mutt behind the ear and resumed his work; he stoked the kindling on the ground under a large pot, pouring the solution into the pot and putting a thermometer inside.

The liquid traveled from the pot into a condenser, down a spiral of copper pipe, continued farther away from the heat source, and finally reached a large glass keg that it slowly drizzled into. Abe watched the liquid drip. He took the wooden spoon and moved it close to the drops, catching several. He brought the liquid to his lips and gave it a try. He flinched again but smiled even wider than before.

"Hoo-hoo. There we go," he chuckled and let the spoon fall to his side as he shook his head.

Chip, despite Abe's warning, got close to the spoon and managed a lick of the moonshine. Instantly, the dog sneezed and backed away from the still.

"See? I told you it was too strong," Abe scolded and shook the spoon at the old dog. "You'd think you'd know better by now."

Chip snorted and shook his head, his ears flopping about. He slunk away and plopped down in the dirt, pouting.

Abe gave the dog no more mind and returned to his work. The stilling process continued, Abe stoking the flames and monitoring the progress. Happy with his production, he stepped back and appreciates the alchemy of it all. With a satisfied nod, he turned and walked back down the short path to his shack, Chip at his heels.

Inside, Abe placed a fresh log in the stove. He opened one of the cupboards and pulled out a rusty tin of coffee beans, prepared to make some coffee. As he clanked the tin on the countertop and reached for a spoon, Chip's ears perked up just a moment before a loud, insistent knocking came from the front door that made Chip begin barking and scurry to the door. Abe frowned at the sound and wiped his hands on his pants before moving to the entrance of his home.

"Okay, okay! I'm coming, I'm coming!" Chip barked on and pawed at the door. Abe shoved the dog aside as the knocking continued. "Allright, that's enough, Chip. Shit. Easy. I'm coming! Down, boy!"

Chip obeyed and sat on his rear, his tail wagged side-to-side in a floor-sweeping flurry, his eyes locked on the knob as Abe reached for it.

The door opened up to find a rail-thin man in his mid-forties in dirty overalls and a wide-brimmed hat. Though his name would suggest otherwise, Marshall Banks was not a lawman. He was a bootlegger too – a delivery man and long-time friend of Abe's. Where Abe was keen and confident, Marshall was an anxious man with a nervous twitch. Where Abe's eyes were keen and focused, Marshall's were watery and wide. Regardless of their differences, Marshall smiled seeing Abe, and the old man smiled in return.

"You're here," Marshall said.

"Why wouldn't I be?" Abe replied.

"It's been a week. I thought you might still be on your supply run, or maybe you'd finally been caught," the thinner man's voice shook with relief.

"Ha," Abe grunted. "Never." He clapped Marshall on the shoulder and squeezed, a brotherly gesture. "Now, you knock like that, I'd think your house was on fire. Come on in. Just put some coffee on." With that, he turned back to his stove.

Marshall entered and shut the door. Chip immediately rose and put his front paws on the Marshall's chest, licking the man's face. "Good to see you too, Chip," he said and patted the dog back to the floor. "You just get back?"

"Yep, and already cooking."

"Good," Marshall said.

At the counter, Abe poured two mugs and the pair sat at the small table. "How's Emily?" Abe asked as they sat.

"She's good," Marshall said. "Stevie's got a bit of colic. Been keeping her up most nights. How's your boy?"

Abe doesn't look at his friend. He waved a dismissive hand at the question. "He's fine. Send Emily my best."

Marshall nodded, knowing not to press the issue.

"Now, why you hammering my door down?" Abe asked and set his mug on the table.

Shifting anxiously in his creaking chair, Marshall set his mug down as well.

"I was hoping you'd have the shipment ready?"

Abe laughed; it was a bark of a laugh, as worn as the rest of the old man, but still full of good humor. "Ha-ha! I just got in not an hour ago. Rose ain't that hard a taskmaster."

"Easy for you to say. You've never seen that look she's got." Marshall mimicked a harsh, wide-eyed glare.

Abe chuckled amused and shrugged. "No, can't say I have."

"I'm being serious, Abe. You remember Rodriguez? The guy I used to run for?"

"Spanish fella. Sure."

"Yeah, he botched up a shipment - a big one. Biggest of the year. And the Boss sent Big Jake to take everything he owned and burned his place down."

Abe shook his head and waved another dismissive hand. "Rodriguez was as honest as a wooden nickel, and Boss Rose knew it. She respects me, I respect her. Besides, I've always been on time.

"I know. I know," Marshall said and took a sip of his coffee. After the sip, he bit his lip and looked at his friend nervously. "When you think it'll be ready?"

Abe exhaled, getting annoyed by Marshall's persistence. "You're an impatient man, Marshall. Whiskey is an art. Art takes time."

"Art. Right," Marshall said. "I just wanna be sure I make my deadlines. I like my things and my home just fine as they are."

With a wink, Abe raised his mug in a toast to himself and his good luck. "Never been late. Don't mean to start now."

Not reassured, Marshall sighed. "Well… okay."

"A little more anxious than normal, ain'tcha?"

Marshall sighed heavily and leaned back in his chair. Abe only then noticed how tired his friend appeared. "New route this time. We had to change boats over to the Malahat, and it's not gonna wait, you know."

Abe made a contemplative noise and leaned back in his own chair thoughtfully. "Hm. The captain on the payroll, right?"

"The first mate," Marshall corrected.

"They'll wait. It'll be fine."

Shaking his head, Marshall sighed anxiously, "You don't know that."

"Yes, I do. Come on." Abe rose from his chair and tucked it back under the table. He stretched and gestured to the backdoor.

Marshall got up and followed his confident friend outside, the sounds of the still creeping into the home.

By lantern light, Marshall inspected the still; the kegs of Abe's whiskey stacked neatly to the side, ready for collecting. Abe picked one up and offered it to the other. Marshall took it, popped the lid, and took a draw. Coughing and laughing at the same time, Marshall said, "Hoo-hoo! Woo, Abe!"

"See? Art," Abe replied proudly.

Marshall set the sample container down. "So, it'll be ready before tomorrow night then, eh?"

"Trust me. Once Boss Rose gets a taste of this new batch, she won't be able to stop thanking you for your services."

Marshall exhales once more, trying to relax, as Abe moves to his still and tenderly runs his hand over it.

CHAPTER TWO

Deep purple bled to red and orange as the sun crawled over the forest and swamp passing the night into day. The world turned, and the clouds drifted through the sky. The day passed in silence, and night fell once more. The world turned and the clouds drifted through the firmament.

As the new evening stretched over the island, a rickety rowboat glided through the dark waters toward a small dock on the shore, and Marshall Banks raised his flickering lantern to light his approach. Standing on the dock, Abe and Chip waited. Behind them on the rocky beach, Abe's truck sat loaded with his kegs of moonshine whiskey.

"You haven't un-loaded yet?" Marshall called out as his boat bobbed through the water and closed the last feet to the dock. "The Malahat isn't going to wait forever."

"And my back isn't what it used to be," Abe replied at the admonishment.

Marshall tied his boat to the pier and hopped up next to Chip, patting the dog aside. "Just drop 'em wherever," he said about the barrels. "I'll get them in the boat."

Abe unlatched the back of his truck and began rolling the kegs one by one to the dock. Marshall took them and placed them gently into the wooden craft. By the sight of it, one wouldn't assume the old boat could bare the weight, but like the old men themselves, it was stronger than it looked.

The task complete, Marshall grew considerably more at ease. He wiped his brow and thanked his friend, "Thanks Abe. If I don't see you before then, Merry Christmas."

"Same to you. Autumn held on a good long time this year. That cold snap is going to come fast. Here." Abe reached out and handed Marshall a mason jar full of his whiskey. "Merry Christmas."

Marshall grinned widely at the sight of the jar. "Thanks, Abe. I really appreciate it."

"Be safe. Don't drink it until you get home."

Marshall nodded as Abe gave the rowboat a shove away from the dock, sending it back out into the dark waters. He stood and watched Marshall vanish and then clicked his tongue for Chip to follow him back to the truck.

The front porch of Abe's shack sat under a portion of roof, protecting the old man from the afternoon sun as it pushed through the canopy of thick trees. Abe sat in his rocking chair and looked out at the swampland before his home. He chewed the end of his pipe, the edges of the chamber stained from countless smokes. He placed a lit match into the chamber and inhaled with gentle puffs. A pop of smoke came from his lips and a thin trail of smoke began to drift from the end of the pipe.

He gripped the stem and held the pipe aloft while lifting his legs onto an apple box. From just beside his feet, music played softly from his radio which sat on another box. "Alone at Last" by Ted Fio Rito and Gus Kahn warbled from the speaker:

I just can't believe it's true,
Here we are alone, we two.
I have waited all my life, it seems,
To tell my dreams to you!

There was I, waiting all alone,
Wondering why I was all alone.
Wondering when I would find you, dear;
You were here, oh so far though so near!

There we met, and we've never known
What it means, being all alone.
Hold me close, time is flying fast,
Here we are, all alone at last!

Ah, there was I, waiting all alone,
Wondering why I was all alone.
Wondering when I would find you, dear;
You were here, oh so far though so near!

There we met, and we've never known
What it means, being all alone.
Oh, hold me close, time is flying fast,
Here we are, all alone at last!

Chip lay a short distance away, dozing in the afternoon light. Abe grinned dreamily at the tune. "You know, Chip, it doesn't get much better than this," the old man said and blew a smoke ring from his wet lips. Chip looked up through half-lidded eyes and then lowered himself back into sleep. Abe rocked in his chair and soaked in the crisp, peaceful day without a care in the goddamn world.

CHAPTER THREE

The morning sun shone brilliantly over the white-capped waves of the Pacific Ocean as fishing boats made their way out to Sea. A cold wind blew from the North. Winter was approaching with a fishing trawler cutting through the waves toward the harbor. Standing in the warm rays of light yet bundled against the mist of salt water, a young man stared transfixed at the nearing shore of Texada Island.

Harry Calloway had just turned 33, yet behind his bright eyes one might find many more years of experiences beyond those three decades. He had been to war and survived. The depths of his eyes hid many battles and many scars, though it was not easy to see past the lenses of his wire-framed glasses. He had a mop of unruly hair on his head, and a kind face, which was turned to the nearing island anxiously. His future awaited him there on the island he'd spent so many years attempting to escape.

The ship made port and the crew and passengers disembarked, including the young man who walked with a limp in his right leg. He bid the Captain farewell, shouldered his beaten rucksack, and placed the last of his parcels into the basket of a bicycle. He received a fair share of odd glances and taunts from the sailors and fisherman as he departed the harbor riding the bike, but Harry paid them no mind.

On the thin paved road leading deeper into the island, Harry rode straight backed and easily. He let the wind whip around him as he passed under tall evergreens, the crystalline waters just beyond them. Harry smiled, content by the early ride and brisk air. He rode for some distance until he came upon a dirt road. He turned himself onto it, and the bike bounced along. He pulled his bag tighter on his shoulders and gripped the handlebars to maintain his control of the bicycle. The dirt path twisted and turned, and Harry's cheeks began to flush. The air may have been chilled by the arriving winter, but the former soldier was beginning to sweat. Although he was enjoying the ride, he was looking forward to reaching his destination. The path began to grow thinner, and he continued to ride.

Cresting the hill and emerging from the trees, Harry's eyes caught sight of a small shack planted among the trees so tightly, one might not even see it if they weren't looking. The dirt road had become a trail and soon barely even that. The bike wobbled through the trees and finally came to a stop with a squeak of the brakes just before the sagging porch. Harry dismounted, and somewhere within the home, a dog barked.

The lantern and radio still sat on Abe's porch next to the rocking chair, though no music was coming from the old box. A wave of memories came to Harry. He stood there and took a long breath of air. He looked at the old shack and blinked. It was exactly as he had remembered it, if not a bit more tired in appearance, but then again, he thought, hadn't everything grown more tired through these last years? The wind blew and the house creaked. Harry reached down and massaged his right leg, a long-since healed wound causing it to be stiffer than his left leg. Rucksack and parcels in hand, he limped slightly toward the house; the old war wound marred his once-confident stride.

As he reached the porch, he glanced down at the out-of-place radio. Adjusting his items, he picked up the radio. He turned to face the door and paused, realizing he no longer had a free hand. He set the radio back down, and knocked on the door.

The barking of the dog returned along with a gruff baritone shout, "Just a minute! I'm coming! Settle down, Chip!"

The door opened, and Abraham looked upon his son for the first time in nearly ten years. The two men stood without saying a word. Chip glanced from his master to Harry and back again. Tired of waiting, the dog jumped up and placed his paws on Harry's chest, nearly knocking the younger man over.

"Hey! Easy there, Chip! Easy!" Abe shouted and pulled the animal back.

Harry laughed, pleased by the old dog's greeting. Abe shoved Chip back into the house to no avail. The dog kept trying to get around Abe's legs, barking joyfully.

"You made it," Abe said with an uncharacteristically soft smile. He looked his son up and down and shook his head. "My God, look at you. You haven't changed one bit."

Harry laughed at his father. "Dad, it's been a long time. I'm sure I've changed quite a bit."

They looked at one another for a moment longer, neither quite sure what to say or do, until Abe stepped forward and clapped Harry on the shoulder and gave him an awkward, half-hearted pseudo-hug while Harry still held all of his items.

"Merry Christmas," Abe said lamely as he stepped back. "Well, in a few weeks anyway."

"Merry Christmas, Dad," Harry said and tossed a glance over his shoulder adding, "Anyone gonna let Mother Nature know what month it is?"

"Hell no," Abe grunted. "I'll take this over the freeze any day. Here, let me take your bags. Come on in. I just finished making breakfast." Abe took the parcels from his son and guided him into the shack.

Inside was cozy, the stove open and a warm glow of a log offering heat. On top of it a skillet of breakfast popping and sizzling, Harry was grateful for the heat. His body warmth had subsided and he was getting chilly from his damp shirt and pants. Abe carried most of Harry's belongings to the bed and set them there. Harry took in the old house, Abe had made an effort to decorate for the coming holiday. He had put up a couple of berry wreaths, a sparse bit of tinsel around a fir little tree, and wood carvings along the windowsills. It was a noble effort, and Harry appreciated it.

The two men stood facing one another for a moment. The confidence and swagger of the bootlegger replaced with an uncertainty, though not without a desire to connect with his estranged son.

Abe stepped forward and extended his hand, which Harry took for a handshake, but the old man pulled him in for another more proper embrace. It was an awkward hug - not something these two frequently did. It lasted only a moment, but Harry felt the love in the instant.

The old man stepped back and cleared his throat. He searched the room for something – anything to talk about, and his gaze landed on the parcels. He could see now that they were presents and packages. Abe cleared his throat a second time and began futzing with his embarrassingly lacking Christmas decorations. "Don't mind the decorations. Place'll look much more festive next week. I asked Emily Marshall to make me some wreaths. Should have those in a few days."

"It's great, Dad," Harry offered kindly. "Truly."

Shrugging, Abe looked away. "Well, anyway, I'm so glad you made it."

"Of course."

"How was the trip? Any troubles?" With a gesture, Abe suggested they sit. Harry pulled off his coat and joined his dad at the kitchen table. They sat.

"No troubles," Harry said. "Not really. The boat to the island was the worst leg."

"Oh, it's nice to slow down and take in the Pacific. The fresh sea air. The waves. I envy you. Can't remember the last time I made it to the mainland. Me and your uncles used to go down to Tacoma. Little pool hall with the finest girls in the North." Abe's gaze shifted as he reminisced about his younger years. "Maybe I oughta get down there again," he said with a grin.

"You should come to Victoria. I would love to show you around," Harry said.

"Hm, maybe," Abe said thoughtfully. "Or you could always come visit me more often."

Harry smiled. "I think one boat trip this year is enough for me. Not sure I have the right kind of sea legs." He patted his bum right leg.

Abe peered at the leg, almost afraid to ask. "How's it? The leg?"

Harry exhaled and shrugged. "Stiff, but it's fine. I get by. It'll flare up once the temperature really drops. Then I hobble around like Frankenstein's monster."

Abe raised an eyebrow. "Not sure I follow you, but whatever you say."

"It's a film. A doctor cooks up this contraption to bring a monster to life–"

Abe snapped his fingers remembering the breakfast. He got up and grabbed the skillet of bacon, eggs, and potatoes. "Sounds exciting," he said as he set everything in front of Harry - coffee, butter, toast. Everything was a touch burnt, but nice.

"If you visit, I can take you to the cinema."

"That's alright," Abe waved a hand and turned back to the stove to pour coffee. "I'm more of a live music man, myself. You point me to a dance hall, and I'll spend the whole night there listening to the band."

"I noticed you still leave your radio on the porch," Harry said and took a bite of bacon. He closed his eyes for a moment to savor the flavor.

Abe sat down again with his coffee. "Oh, that doesn't matter. But thanks."

"It could get stolen."

A laugh. "Out here?" Abe asked blithely. "Whoever takes it is going to take it out of necessity. They can have it, far as I'm concerned."

"You'd just let someone take it?" Harry asked.

"I'll get another," Abe shrugged. "Or whoever'd take it would bring it back. That's life here. You city slickers are a more protective lot. We're a family here."

Harry thought about that. "That's kinda nice. I suppose with more people crammed in one place, there's more crime. Over 30 thousand people all hustling and bustling."

"There you go," Abe felt his point proven. "How can you know your neighbor well enough to let 'em steal your radio when there's 30 thousand of 'em?"

Harry frowned. A need to defend his city rose in his chest and he spoke before he could stop himself from sounding offended. "There's plenty good about Victoria too, Dad. More than one general store, the cinema and theater, rail cars. And people from all over the world. It's nice."

Abe was doubtful. "Mmhmm. Plenty of nice people here. Nicer, I'd bet."

It was an uncomfortable moment, the unfamiliarity between the two men obvious by their feelings about small town life and city life. Harry poked at his meal, the flavors lessened by the tension. Abe sipped his coffee. He cleared his throat.

"There's a lot of people asking about you. We miss you up here, you know."

Harry poked a moment longer at his food. He took several seconds to build to something he'd decided to ask before he'd ever set foot on the ship back on the mainland. An idea had gotten into his head – a desire – and he braced himself for his father's reaction.

"Dad," Harry began. "I'm thinking about staying around again for a spell."

Abe's eyebrows rose and he peered over his coffee mug, mid-sip. "Oh? Even after Christmas?"

Harry kept his eyes on his plate. "Yes, I actually do think it'd be nice to be away from the city for awhile."

Abe lowered his mug and looked at his son, curious.

Harry, eyes still down, held his fork tightly. "I tried re-enlisting, but my leg…" he trailed off.

Abe could see the pain in his son's heart as clear as the frown on the young man's face. Abe grunted and offered bitterly, "Hmph. Army doesn't mind men hurting themselves for the cause, but they don't want you back after they've used you up."

Harry lifted his shoulders and let them drop. "The War's long over. They've let plenty of men go. Whether we want to go or not."

Another moment of silence passed.

This time, Harry broke it by clearing his throat and saying timidly, "Well, anyway, I thought I'd stay around. Help you out a bit."

Abe looked at his son, proud of the boy, mad to see him mistreated, and happy he's seated before him. "I'd love you to.

Been trying to get you back here for years, boy! You're always welcome. It's a bit small, if don't mind."

Harry finally raised his gaze to his father as Abe hopped up and moved to his pantry grabbing a jar of moonshine. "This calls for a toast, I think!" Abe cheered.

Harry let out a long sigh. He was not pleased to see the jar of booze. "Dad," he said, "it's a little early for that."

Abe blew through his lips and poured out his coffee, emptying his mug. He grabbed a second glass and filled both with the moonshine. He sat and passed one to Harry. "My boy's come home. It's Christmas. Plenty of reasons for a sip."

Harry frowned. "I want to be clear, Dad. When I said help out, I didn't mean with…" he waved a hand over the mug and gestured to the backdoor. "The business."

Abe raised an eyebrow, his confident swagger returned. "Well, you won't have to worry about none of that. Chip and I have managed on our own for this long, after all."

Harry sighed once more. He shook his head at his father. "Okay, as long as you understand. I want to be here with you, but I don't want to be mixed up with any of your nonsense. If you get picked up, I don't want to be implicit in your crimes."

"Haha! "Implicit." Listen to that five dollar word!" He raised his mug. "You don't know nothing, you can't say nothing if Johnny Law comes a-knocking."

Harry continued to frown. "Yes, but my reputation..."
Or: my reputation – "

"Will be just fine, boy. When the day comes I gotta answer for my sins, I'll answer to St. Peter all by myself. Now, a toast."

Harry opened his mouth to say something else, but he didn't bother. He raised his glass, shaking his head, amused. "You always were stubborn."

Abe clinked his mug against Harry's toasting, "To stubborn men! The old fools and the apples that didn't fall far from the tree." Abe took a hearty gulp of his drink.

Harry attempted to do the same but after only a sip began coughing violently. "Ho-lee-!"

Abe launched into a great, big belly laugh while patting his gasping son on the back.

CHAPTER FOUR

Prohibition consumed Seattle during these years, igniting a war among the gangs that played out in the streets, waterways, and even town hall. Skirting around the law, the Coast Guard, and the zealous Assistant Director of the Seattle Prohibition Bureau, William Whitney, was no simple feat, but many rose to the challenge. The law could barely control the streets, and when former lawman Roy Olmstead turned his back on his oath and became the King of the Seattle Bootleggers, things only got worse. His partner in crime Johnny Schnarr ran liquor down from Canada and revolutionized the speedboat industry. Frank Gatt, a south Seattle restaurateur, started the state's biggest moonshining operation. All of these men battled one another in bloody conflicts that ended in many deaths. But while these gangland kings and seaside warlords raged against one another and the government machine, one woman set herself above them all. One woman sat in the shadows and watched these small men stupidly battle one another while she sliced off piece after piece of the bootlegger's pie for herself. While gangsters fought to be king of the American Northwest, Rose O'Chauncey became the Queen.

Standing on the upper floor of her oceanside warehouse staring out the wall length window, Prohibition Rose dipped her pinky finger into her crystal tumbler of whiskey. Rose was an attractive woman of 40 with dangerous amber eyes and fiery red hair. Her expensive dress was tailored to her curves, and her hair was tightly lifted away from her face. She touched the wet tip of her finger to her lips and slowly ran it over her bottom lip as she contemplated the bobbing lights along the dock. Her dock.

The lanterns glowing in the night were from the Malahat, a Canadian fishing boat transporting her newest shipment of kegs from the North. She squinted, making out the shadowy forms of her men helping unload the shipment from the boat. Among them was a thin man she had grown to tolerate, Marshall Banks. Even in the dark, she could tell it was him by the way he nervously paced, a drastic difference from the statuesque way Rose stood at her window. She licked her lower lip, setting her glass down on the sill.

"Easy now. You break any of those, and there'll be more than hell to pay," Marshall warned the sailor carrying the last of the kegs from the Malahat.

"Oh yeah?" the sailor asked with annoyance in his tone. And who's the devil, eh? You?" He laughed along with his fellow sailors, but as he turned back to face Marshall, his laughter ceased and his face grew pale. He lowered his head.

Marshall peered about to see what had stopped the man and found Rose O'Chauncey standing a short distance away with her hands behind her back. Her no-nonsense glare was enough to freeze any man in his tracks. Hell, her powerful gaze was enough to make a man forget his own name.

"Sorry, boss," the sailor muttered and quickly headed back to the Malahat.

Rose offered a tilt of her chin, the only acknowledgement she gave any of the sailors. She held out her hand, a white glove wrapped around her slender fingers, to the man beside her, Jake Edwards, a deceptively well-built man in his sixties towering over six-feet-tall and nearly just as broad shouldered. Jake was Rose's second. Jake handed Rose one of the small jars of moonshine from the fresh shipment. Rose took a step toward Marshall.

"Smooth sailing?" she asked.

Marshall wiped the sweat off his forehead with his sleeve and anxiously nodded to his Boss and then looked away. He allowed himself the briefest of glances at Jake but quickly averted his eyes from the muscular man as well, intimidated more by him than the smoky woman. This made Rose happy. She wanted to see fear from her subordinates. She wanted them afraid of her or afraid of her muscle. Either way, she wanted them scared.

"Yes, ma'am. No trouble at all," Marshall squeaked. "This is is the last of it. Every drop accounted for."

"Did you get the rest of Abe Calloway's supply?"

"Yes, ma'am. This is it right here." Marshall grabbed one of Abe's mason jars and offered it to Rose.

Jake stepped forward and snatched the jar from Marshall much more swiftly than necessary. Marshall recoiled. Jake handed the jar to his boss.

Rose cracked the seal and lifted it to her nose. She inhaled it with closed eyes, the corners of her lips lifting ever-so-slightly in satisfaction. She tilted the jar and slowly took the tiniest of sips. What followed was a savory groan of delight. "Ah, that'll get my customers going. Always perfection. Always good. Very good. Jake, be sure a crate of this makes it to my girls for the VIPs."

Jake nodded and stepped to the side to allow Rose to continue her conversation with Marshall. She walked closer to the thin man making him visibly nervous. "Your man knows what he's doing," Rose said.

"One of the best, boss," Marshall replied with a tremble in his voice.

Rose looped her arm through Marshall's and turned him on the spot. "Walk with me, Banks." She wasn't asking. They began strolling toward the warehouse. Jake followed just behind them, omnipresent. Rose went on, "Now that your shipment is in, I have use for you elsewhere. Have you heard the news of Big Jimmy B?"

Marshall swallowed dryly. "No, ma'am."

Rose sighed exaggeratedly sad. "I'm pained to say that Big Jim died last week."

"Oh wow. That's a shame. What happened?" Marshall inquired.

"Lead poisoning," Rose said.

Marshall swallowed again. He knew that meant a sudden and impactful death.

Rose continued, "He was a good man, but we must focus on the now. His eldest son wants to take over Jim's route. I want you to head to his place. Bring me the latest batch. The boy should be done by now."

Marshall nodded, compliant. "Yes, ma'am."

Rose stopped and faced Marshall. She reached up, patted him on the cheek, and smiled banally. He shivered. A memory flashed through his head.

An employee who had stolen from Boss Rose.

Jake chopping the man's hands off.

The man cursing Rose's soul.

A bullet through his head.

Rose forcing Marshall to help Jake dispose of the body.

Marshall swallowed dryly and Rose smiled seeing the fear in his face. "Good boy," she said. And with that, she left Marshall standing there as she walked into her warehouse, Jake following just behind.

Shivering from more than just the cold, Marshall backed away; and then, hurried to the Malahat as fast as he could without running.

CHAPTER FIVE

Abe walked in from the back path and his still with a bundle of freshly cut firewood in his arms to find Harry cooking bacon and eggs on the wood stove. "Beautiful morning. Definitely smell snow in the air. Probably get a good dusting before the New Year. Hopefully, before Christmas even," Abe said as he dropped the armload of wood on the floor beside the stove.

"That'll be nice. Never does feel much like Christmas without a good amount of snow on the ground."

Abe walked to the water basin and washed his hands. "Been a mild winter so far. Made it easier on me out back though. Don't mind that one bit." He shifted to the table and pulled a chair out. Sitting, he took off his boots.

Choosing not to acknowledge the mention of the still, Harry placed a mug on the table beside his father's elbow and poured a hot cup of coffee for the old man. "I'd like a good snowfall," Harry said. "Snow in the city always feels filthy."

Abe picked up the mug and sipped at the hot beverage. "So what's the plan for today? Going to spend some time here? I could use the company. Chip is a wonderful listener, but he's a terrible conversationalist."

Over on the bed, Chip raised his head hearing his name.

"The fishing should be good along the river right now," Abe added.

"I was going to visit the mill. Curt DeBruin and I have been corresponding, and he knows I'm back for the holiday."

Abe smiled fondly. "Curt DeBruin. That little beanpole. How's he doing?"

Harry pulled the other chair from the table and sat across from his dad. He placed plates of eggs and bacon for the both of them. Taking a napkin, he shook it open and placed it on his lap before grabbing a fork and knife. "Foreman now. And they're looking for more hands to finish off the season."

Abe frowned, glancing quickly at Harry's leg sticking out from underneath the table. "Are you sure about that, with your..." he caught himself and tried more tact. "I mean, does he know about it?"

"I can manage," Harry said stubbornly and stabbed a piece of bacon with his fork.

"Yes, but with the saws, the tree stands. That's all going to leave a major strain on your leg. You'll get water on the knee within the first hour."

"I have a brace. It makes it much easier to manage."

Abe stared at his boy unconvinced, managing only a lame, "Okay."

Harry looked into his dad's eyes, and Abe saw the Calloway fire in them, the same determination Abe had everyday of his long life. "Dad, I'll be fine," Harry said.

Abe knew that was the final word on the matter. He shrugged and tucked into his eggs, starting a casual conversation about the fishing conditions of the river just down the way.

Once finished, Harry rose, tossed the last bite of bacon into his mouth, and took his plate and mug to the basin and washed them clean. He pulled on his boots and coat and walked to the front door. Chip rose and let his tongue flop out in hopeful anticipation.

"Sorry, Chip," Harry smiled. "I'll take you for a walk later."

"You're going already?" Abe said, not hiding his disappointment very well.

"I have errands to run."

"What errands?" Abe asked sourly. "You make yourself an escape plan if this didn't work out?"

Harry shook his head at that. "Dad."

They looked at one another. Once again, the tension between the two men thick in the air. Abe picked up his coffee mug and swirled the dregs of it around in a circle just to have something to do. Harry sighed slowly looking at the old man. Maybe coming here wasn't the best idea after all.

"If Curt hires me on, he has a cabin back of the mill. I can stay there for the week. Won't hardly be any walking for me to and from work."

"Fine," Abe said and got out of his chair. He turned his back on Harry and filled his mug again.

Harry looked at his father's back, the distance between them was more than the few meters from the front door to the kitchen area.

"You're coming back for Christmas morning, though, aren't you? Your Gramma would string me up if I didn't bring you over to her."

A tender smile crossed Harry's face. "Of course, Dad."

Abe closed his eyes a moment, realizing just how needy he sounded. He cleared his throat loudly–manly. He turned to face Harry and said, "Well then, alright. Take care of yourself. Mill Road has a few felled trees - funny seeing a bunch of loggers unable to keep the road to a logging mill clear. I'd go out there myself, but I don't drive all that often."

Harry nodded. "Thanks. I'll be careful. Who knows. Maybe that'll be my first task. Clear the road."

Abe smirked. "Maybe."

They looked at one another for a moment longer, neither knowing what to say. Harry broke the silence. "Stay out of trouble, Dad."

"Don't I always?"

Harry gave Chip a pet and nodded halfheartedly. With that, the young man exited, carrying his satchel. Abe watched him go and listened as Harry's footsteps moved ????? across the porch and were soon followed by the crunch of bicycle wheels on dirt. Then, Abe and Chip were all alone once again.

Chip whined at Abe's plate.

Abe shook his head. "Greedy little rascal," he said and set his plate on the floor for his dog.

Wiping his hands on his pants, he walked over to his fishing gear. Two poles rested against the wall, one of them was worn and used, like everything in Abe's life. The other pole was clean and looked almost brand new. Abe's eyes took the two fishing rods in, and his jaw tightened for a moment. "Y'know," he said to Chip or himself, "I don't feel all that much like fishing today." He grabbed his coat and walked out the backdoor to his still.

The sun shone warmly on the frosty land. The trees swayed in the wind. Snow clouds loomed in the distance, slowly creeping toward the island. Harry rolled down the path and onto the paved road. He blew through his lips, slightly exhausted from trekking up the hill to get this far, but glad to now have a smoother ride ahead.

He zipped down the paved road, as trees and brush whipped by him. He took long drinks of air and savored the cleanliness of it all. He smelled the sharp scents of the fir and dogwood trees. The last hints of autumn being chased away by the approaching cold were still beautiful; orange and red of the leaves reflecting into pools of water in the rivers and nearby ocean sparkled through the branches and brush. He came over the peak of a hill, gripping the handlebars on his bike, and allowed gravity to do the work for him; he soared down the hill and couldn't help but smile.

Miles later, Harry rolled up to a logging camp, quite winded from his journey. He dismounted stiffly, his leg bothering him, but he sucked it up and walked into camp.

Three burly men were organizing their gear: saws and axes, rope and twine. Watching over them was a tall, muscular man with a massive, bushy beard. Curt DeBruin was the same age as Harry, but his manly stature and even more manly facial hair made him look ten years older. He adjusted the rifle hanging over his shoulder and talked in a brusk tone to his workers, "We'll finish harvesting the south plot today. And I want a survey of the East. If this weather is going to hold, we can hold off too, but I want an idea of how swiftly we can take it all down."

Harry waited until he was closer to the men to draw attention to himself. He stood tall and did his best to hide his limp. "How about an extra pair of hands?" he called out.

Curt turned to the new voice and lit up the moment his eyes hit his childhood friend. "Harry! Haha! You made it! How are you, my friend?" He closed the distance between them and clapped Harry on the shoulder with one of his meaty, lumberjack hands.

"Good to see you, Curt," Harry grinned, and the two old friends embraced.

Curt stepped back and looked him up and down. "Army life has done you well." He gestured to Harry and spoke to his men. "Boys, you're looking at a genuine veteran of the Great War, and one of the finest spear fishermen I've ever known. Major Harry Calloway."

The workers all nodded and offered greetings respectfully. Two even shook Harry's hand saying, "Good to meet you, Major."

The other man said, "Thank you for your service."

Harry bowed his head gratefully. "Thank you," he said humbly.

"I didn't think you'd come," Curt grinned. "City life that boring? Coming back home to slum it with us tree folk?"

Harry laughed, "Stow it. I'm calling in your favor. You have trees that need coming down. I have strong hands and a firm back. Put me to work."

Curt laughed in return, playfully ribbing Harry, "Ho-ho! A man sees action in the Somme, and he's ready to take on the logging industry, eh?"

A twinge of pain crossed Harry's face for an instant, his mind flashed back to that terrible battle, but he quickly brushed it away and cocked an eyebrow in reply. "Can't be too difficult if you're in charge around here."

Curt grinned wider still and threw an arm over Harry's shoulders pulling him into a headlock. "Think you have what it takes to be a lumberjack, boy? Ha-ha!"

They jostled about for a moment. The other woodcutters smiled, glad to see their boss so cheerful. Harry got free of Curt's huge arms. "Put an ax in my hands, and I'll level the forest."

"Good man," Curt said. "Come on, I'll show you around." He slapped Harry one more time on the shoulder and began walking deeper into the camp. As he walked, he shouted orders to his men, "Alright! Enough farting around. Back to work, you apes."

Harry followed Curt, doing everything in his strength not to limp.

"We can put you in cabin 26," Curt said without giving any notice to Harry.

Harry managed to stay at his friend's side. "Cabin 26. Got it."

With a pat on the butt of his firearm, Curt continued, "I'll get you a rifle. Keep it on yourself at all times, eh?"

"Having some trouble out here?" Harry frowned.

"Not so much with bandits on these islands, but there are some wolves around up the coast."

"How much of a problem are they?" Harry asked and fired a worried glance to the nearby treeline.

Curt lowered his head sadly. "Cecil, Robert's boy. Poor bugger got snowbound deep in the woods near Powell River last winter. Wolves got to him."

"I'm sorry to hear that. I heard the snow was bad. Did they find him?"

Curt nodded. "A few days later when the storm died down. The rest of the boys really took it hard. He was young. Good kid."

They walked in quiet reflection, Curt's thoughts going back to the lost man, Harry's memory drifted back to the Great War once more. Battlefields of mud and snow, bloody trenche, and the anguished cries of young men dying. A dark sky filled with smoke and ash hung over them, and the cold hand of death clawed its way into every corner of the dying world. Harry shivered and spoke in a low, somber tone, "I know what that feels like, losing a member of the team - a friend."

Curt replied respectfully, "I know. I know."

They walked a bit and came upon some uneven ground. Harry's right foot caught a rock and he winced as his ankle turned. Curt glanced and finally noticed Harry's limp.

"What's with the leg?" he asked casually.

Harry flushed but shook it off. "Oh, it's a bit stiff. Nothing serious."

Curt eyed Harry suspiciously. He stopped and faced him. He took the butt of his rifle and tapped the side of Harry's pants. There is a soft THUNK-THUNK. Harry closed his eyes, a touch embarrassed. He pulled up his pant leg to reveal a brace. Curt whistled, impressed.

"Say now, that's a swell looking doohickey," Curt said.

"Nice, isn't it? It's like my knee's brand new. Most of the time, I don't even know I'm wearing it."

Curt whistled again. "What will they think of next? It's fantastic!"

"Thanks."

Curt rubbed his stubbled chin in consideration.

Harry interjected nervously, "It's not a problem, honestly. I'm as mobile as anyone. Don't ask me to do any sprinting, but I can pull my own weight." He attempted to smile confidently, and pointed at Curt's belly. "Might even be more fit than you. You're a little wider than I remember."

"Ha!" Curt laughed and patted his stomach. "It's my hibernation weight. You'll need some too, or at the very least you'll need to grow that beard out. You look like a baby with that smooth face."

"Hey now," Harry grinned. "I haven't shaved in two weeks."

They both laughed.

"Alright, Hare. If you think you can hold your own, I trust you. Welcome to the team." Curt thrust his hand forward and gripped Harry's tightly. Harry smiled in great relief and pride. He was determined to prove himself.

Curt put his arm over Harry's shoulder and guided him toward the forest. As they went, Curt began to sing in a booming voice:

"When Winter comes, the winter wild that hill and wood shall slay;
When trees shall fall and starless night devour the sunless day;
When wind is in the deadly East, then in the bitter rain
I'll look for thee, and call to thee; I'll come to thee again!"

Harry raised his voice and joined in the jovial song:

"When Winter comes, and singing ends; when darkness falls at last;
When broken is the barren bough, and light and labour past;
I'll look for thee, and wait for thee, until we meet again:
Together we will take the road beneath the bitter rain!"

And they finished the number together as they disappeared into the trees, two old friends reunited.

"Together we will take the road that leads into the West,

And far away will find a land where both our hearts may rest."

CHAPTER SIX

An eagle soared over the treetops, its incredible eyes sweeping the terrain for prey which was growing scarce as winter drew ever closer. The weather was still holding, but the looming clouds hung in the distance slowly creeping closer like an inevitable beast consuming the last remnants of Autumn. The eagle swooped, and continued its hunt.

From the porch of his shack, Abe watched the majestic bird and puffed on his pipe. The radio chirped beside him, the Isham Jones Orchestra launching into another big band number. Abe tapped his foot along with the tune. Chip, asleep at Abe's side, lifted his head with his ears perked. A moment later, a truck rumbled into view on the thin path from the main road.

Abe set his pipe aside and stood. He looped his thumbs into his belt and squinted at the approaching vehicle. The truck came to a squeaky stop a short distance away, and Marshall emerged. "Morning," he greeted his friend.

"How was it?" Abe asked.

"Uneventful," Marshall lied, and Abe could tell. Marshall held up an envelope and waged it at Abe. "I come bearing gifts."

Abe accepted the envelope and peeled it open to find a thick collection of bills. "You take your cut?"

"Yessir," Marshall said and scratched Chip behind the ear. Abe returns to his rocking chair. Marshall sits in the empty chair beside the radio. "You were right about Boss Rose. She loved your latest batch."

"Of course she did. Best moonshine in the West," Abe winked.

Marshall reached into his back pocket and pulled out another bundle of papers. "Got a letter for you."

Abe took the proffered envelope and ripped it open. It was from Harry. He read it slowly.

"Why's Harry sending you letters?" Marshall asked. I thought he was staying here with you."

"That's what I thought. Guess he was eager to get out there and make better use of his time than spending it here with his old man and Chip. He took some work over at the mill. He took one of the cabins there."

"The mill?" Marshall scratched his chin. "Thought his leg was lame."

"It's not bad. Seems it's holding up well enough," Abe said and kept reading. "And he hasn't had to shoot nothing yet."

"Hm," Marshall intoned. "Good news all around, then." Marshall pulled out a tobacco tin and paper to roll a cigarette. "Shame though."

Abe sighed with overt disappointment, "Yeah. It was hard enough having him in Victoria, but now that he's back here on the island, it's almost more difficult. He's so close, but it feels like he's farther away."

Marshall stuck a freshly rolled cigarette between his lips and lit it with a match. He took a draw and blew smoke into the air. "I felt the same way when my brother left for the mines. It's not like he was that far away, but he was always too busy for me. We used to do the sled races every New Year, but once he was working - pfft - no time for the dogs."

Chip raised his head. Marshall pet it.

"Well, maybe if I were sledding dogs he'd be more willing to stick around," Abe said and tightened his lips into a thin line.

Marshall read the expression. "Your business?" he asked knowingly.

Abe raised his brow. "Don't think he approves."

Gasping dramatically, Marshall declared, "Doesn't approve of his father, the heroic savior of the thirsty masses up and down the Pacific Coast?"

Abe laughed and waved a hand at his friend. "He's a good kid. Always been. That's why he made such a good soldier."

Marshall thought for a moment, his nervousness returning a bit. "You don't think he'd tell anyone, do you?"

"No, no, no. Not Harry. He's a fine soldier, but he's a good son first," Abe assured.

"War changes a man, Abe. You seen some of the veterans around here."

"Not Harry. He's strong. Stubborn."

Marshall tilted his head. "Wonder where he got that from."

The corner of Abe's mouth turned up in a puckish grin. He raised a fist to his friend and shook it playfully threatening his friend. "Same place he got his grit. What of it?"

Marshall raised his hands in submission. "Alright, alright." He took a final sip of his cigarette and snubbed it out on the bottom of his shoe. He rose. "I'd better get going. Emily says you two should come for Christmas Eve. She's making a feast, and she'll need as many bellies as we can muster to eat it all."

"Lord knows I would love that, but I promised Bessie I'd bring Harry over to her."

"The mother-in-law?" Marshall pressed his lips together tightly.

"Yep," Abe sighed heavily.

Marshall exhaled, intimidated by the mere mention of the woman. "How's that old bat still flapping around?"

Abe chuckled and peered around in mock worry. "Don't let her hear you say that."

Marshall laughed in response, but quickly cringed and he couldn't stop himself from looking around nervously. "She hasn't been happy with you since Theodora passed, eh?"

Abe laughed. "Oh, it's been much longer than that. Bessie never thought I was good enough for Theodora. If I wasn't perfect, I wasn't anything to her."

Abe smiled at memories of long ago, when he and the love of his life held one another. His thoughts found Theodora, his perfect wife. He saw her petite frame and long hair tied up in a messy bun, her hazel eyes taking him in. He saw her smile, her teeth so perfectly aligned. He felt her touch, her small hands holding him tightly. He laid with her in the morning glow. He held her closely, felt her love every moment of everyday of their lives together. He saw her walking from her family's estate to climb into his carriage and ride off into the night. He saw sunsets on the beach and staring into one another's eyes. He adored her. He loved her beyond reason, and inexplicably, she loved him in return. They had lived with that love for far too short of a lifetime. She had been taken from the Earth not long after Harry's fifth birthday. Abe's face fell, his heart pained as the vision of Theodora drifted away.

"Harry's another story in Bessie's eyes," Abe sighed. "Woman adores him."

"Well," Marshall said. "If you survive, you come by for a good meal from Em."

"Your wife's an angel, my friend. Off with you, then. Be safe."

Marshall gave Abe a wave as he walked to his truck. He climbed in, brought the engine to life, and rumbled away, back the way he came down the thin, tree lined path.

Abe relit his pipe and rocked back in his chair. He looked off at the horizon, still another eagle swooped through the clouds, and the old man's thoughts drifted back to his lost love.

CHAPTER SEVEN

Curt DeBruin had not been in battle, though he had been to war. He had trained with the Canadian Army, and he knew how to fight, but his true skills had been with the trees. In a world of industry where so much was now manmade, it was easy to forget that during the Great War, there had been a large demand for wood. At the height of the War, it was believed that every soldier required the equivalent of five trees. The lumber was needed for their housing, for their ammunition crates, and crates to store and transport food; wood was found in tanks and other equipment. Wood was needed for explosives, gun stocks, ships, and factories. And painfully, wood was needed for their coffins.

The Canadian Forestry Corps was a military unit of the Canadian Army. The original plan was that Canada would gather lumber to be sent overseas, but space aboard merchant ships was limited, so a new plan was formed. The lumberjacks of The Great White North were sent instead. These men set aside their rifles and bayonets for their axes and saws and harvested the trees of Scotland.

24,000 woodcutters served in the Canadian Forestry Corp until the end of the War, and Curt DeBruin had been one of those brave men. He had cut countless trees, and he had come home. Now, he stood overseeing the harvesting of the forests of Texada Island watching his childhood friend in admiration. Curt knew that Harry Calloway had been in battle. He knew that Harry had been injured and yet continued to fight. He watched as Harry even now continued to fight – fight the limp in his leg. Fight the stigma of those who'd returned from Europe changed. Curt had served with many great lumberjacks, and he had known many great soldiers. He was looking at a man who was both.

"Timber!" Harry shouted. He was off on his own working a section of forest. He rested his axe on his shoulder and stepped aside as his last tree of the day fell to the forest floor with a deafening crunch flopping against other trees. Harry wiped his brow and adjusted his spectacles on the bridge of his nose. He prepared to limb the tree. He walked the length of the felled monstrosity and surveyed his work. As he reached the top of the tree where the branches thinned, something caught his eye just within the trunks of the still standing trees nearby. He paused, his breath catching in his throat.

Laying among the branches was a pair of boots. Legs stuck out from the tree, leaves and dirt obstructing them. Harry froze in shock, unsure as to what he was looking at – desperate for it to not be what his eyes and heart told him it was the moment he saw it. He moved to investigate, and swallowed dryly as his fears were confirmed.

It was the rotting body of a man lying in a trench.

"Oh God," Harry gasped and stepped back. His foot caught a root. He lost his footing and he tumbled backwards to the ground. Clamoring away from the body, he shouted, "H-hey! Hey! We got a man down over here! Medic! Medic!" he shouted on instinct.

Curt and two other came racing over to Harry. One of the workers helped him to his feet, and Harry winced from the pain in his leg.

Bending down, Curt pulled debris away from the man's face, which surprisingly still held its feature, though the dead man's skin was grey and sucken. He was not someone Curt recognized though.

"Been out her for some time," Curt said to the others, his voice level. "You okay, Hare?"

"Y-yeah. I'm good. I'm..." his voice was shaking. "Just relieved I didn't just kill a man, but yeah, I'm fine."

Curt looked once more at the body, the smell of the man was pungent and sour. Curt covered his mouth and nose and rose. "We'd better call the Mounties."

Harry sat on the bed of a logging truck a distance from the body, still shaken by the situation. Images of the trenches of Europe swam through his mind's eye, and he shuddered at the haunting memories of the endless piles of dead men he'd borne witness to. Curt was speaking with three Mounties as they inspected the body; the man had been brought out of the trees and laid covered by a blanket on a tarp. Other workers had gathered out of morbid curiosity. Curt shook the Mounties' hands and walked to Harry with a dour expression. "Near as they can tell, it's just some hunter," Curt said and sat beside Harry. "Must've gotten lost and froze or starved in the night. Damn unlucky. Half mile from the mill. Poor bastard only needed to keep walking."

Harry stared at the lump under the blanket and repeated numbly, "Poor bastard."

Curt could see how shaken his friend was. "You okay?"

Harry sat quietly. He nodded a little. "Yeah," he offered unconvincingly.

Curt patted his pal's back. "You've been a big help these past couple of days. You've put us on a great pace to finish the year off. Why don't you take the rest of the week off. Start Christmas early with your pa."

Harry blinked at that, letting it settle in his mind. He cleared his throat and shook his head. "It's fine, Curt. I'm okay, really."

"I'm sure you are, but I want you to take the time off." Curt chewed on his tongue trying to find the words. He didn't know how to address the shellshock. He pointed at Harry's leg as an excuse. "You should give that a rest. Two days was pushing it. I can tell."

Harry is struck by this, offended by the accusation. He stood abruptly and said coldly, "My leg is fine."

Curt looked down, ashamed to have said anything. He couldn't bring himself to look at his friend, but he knew he had to push on. He looked Harry directly in the eye. "How about I stick you inside - work the desk for me. Plenty of paperwork to keep you busy for a few days." Before Harry could protest, Curt went on quickly, "Just 'till the 26th. Then, the kid gloves come off. I'm planning on working you so damn hard, you'll be cursing my name to the Devil and God."

Harry stared at his old friend. There was an understanding. Curt meant no offense intended; he was doing his best, and Harry accepted that with a gentle nod. "Thanks, Curt."

Curt simply nodded in return.

CHAPTER EIGHT

Abe walked into the local speakeasy and took a moment to scan the illicit establishment before finding Marshall seated at a corner table already indulging in a beverage and a meaty burger. Abe walked through the place. It was a small tavern, but it was filled with patrons: loggers, fishermen, and townies. It was a lively group of debaucherous types looking to wet their whistles despite the mandated Prohibition in Canada. Music blared from a small three piece band jamming in the corner on a guitar, drum, and upright bass. Abe bobbed his head in tempo with the soundtrack of the establishment.

In addition to the music, came a loud, rowdy din. At the one end of the bar, a younger man named Samuel Shea was barking in laughter with several friends. They didn't appear to be loggers or fishermen; Abe considered their rough appearance. They were the kind of fellas that would make you cross to the other side of the street if you saw them coming. Not the most uncommon of folks in a speakeasy.

Speakeasies were quite common during these dry years, though this was the only one located on Texada Island. In Irish and British dialect, a speak softly shop meant a smuggler's den, but here and now, the term referred to an unlicensed saloon and the slang came from the simple practice of speaking quietly about such a place in public, or when inside it, so as not to alert the police and neighbors.

Abe pulled up a chair at Marshall's table and took a seat. He raised his fingers and snapped with a short, soft whistle to get the attention of the barmaid, Sara. She waved in response and in no time at all, she swooped over to Abe with a tall glass of beer and a plate with a plump burger set in a bed of fries and gravy. Abe thanked Sara and tucked into his meal.

"Ah, I've been waiting all day for this," Abe said and chewed the juicy meat.

Marshall raised his glass. "Amen, brother." He took a long swig and smacked his lips.

The two friends discussed the next shipment Abe was preparing and when they'd have a chance to meet up for billiards or fishing. After several more bites of his burger, Abe took a sip of his beer and winced.

"What's the matter?" Marshall grinned. "That's one of the best brews on the island."

"If that's true, I need to start brewing beer too." Abe considered the drink.

"Don't think Rose would mind that one bit."

Abe attempted another sip and shook his head. It was no good. "Ugh. Tastes like piss."

Marshall snorted, "Well, given what it's made of…"

The door to the bar banged open and a tall, thin man breezed into the place. Abe glanced up to see the figure standing there and frowned. Marshall turned to see who'd entered, and he grimaced as well.

Fergus Bradshaw was in his late twenties and built broad. His shoulders were wide and strong. He had a cocky swagger about him. His confidence came from his family name. His father had been the late and much respected moonshiner Jimmy Bradshaw. Fergus knew his name carried weight in the moonshiner community. Beside him were his two trusted friends, Earl Martin and RJ Johnson, both of them as mean-faced as their hotheaded friend. Those nearest to the entrance who had seen their arrival offered wary glances that quickly turned to huge smiles when Bradshaw declared in a booming voice, "Next round is on me, boyos!"

A cheer rose over the establishment in celebration of some of the finest words one could utter in a bar, even back then.

Bradshaw and his men walked in and made their way to the bar. Marshall cringed at the sight of the kid and shifted to keep his back to Fergus, not wanting to be noticed.

"Who's the kid?" Abe frowned watching the display of bravado from Bradshaw as patrons gathered around him.

"Jimmy B's boy," Marshall said.

Abe got a good look at Bradshaw's face. "I don't see it."

"More hair. About 50 kilos lighter."

Abe scrutinized Fergus as the young man revelled in the attention of the men all around him, basking in his popularity. "You gentlemen get a good look at my newest toy?" he bellowed. "Won it off an Italian in a game of cards down in Portland." Fergus brandished a set of keys. "Duesenberg Model J Derham Tourster. The finest car in the world! Who wants a ride!"

The crowd cheered.

"How'd a fella as fat and as humble as Jimmy produce a blowhard like that?" Abe asked.

Marshall replied, "He just inherited Jimmy's route and run. Throwing money around like he wants to be caught."

Abe did not approve. "His stuff any good?" he asked.

"I don't know; he hasn't sold much around here, but Boss Rose seems to like him. On my last trip, she had me pick up his shipment. He was a cocky son of a bitch even then, and Jimmy had just passed. Looks like he's gotten worse."

"I didn't know Jimmy had a boy," Abe said, still watching Bradshaw.

"He was living in the States, I hear. Virginia."

"Ah. American. That explains it."

"Hey! My mother was American," Marshall said sourly.

"My condolences," Abe smirked and winked.

"Keep it up, and I might forget how much of a cut you get next shipment," Marshall retorted.

Abe snickered and picked up his beer. In the moment, he'd forgotten its quality and took a drink, immediately regretting it and grimacing.

At the bar, Bradshaw pulled a wad of cash out of his jacket the size of a baseball. Among the cheering patrons, Samuel's eyebrows raised at the site of the money.

Abe shook his head. "Typical rube, flashing his money around."

"Not like your jealous," Marshall suggested with his tone.

Abe scoffed, "Jealous of some young buck? Bite your tongue."

"I don't know. He's already in Rose's good graces. Maybe he's worth keeping an eye on."

"I ain't worried. Rose knows I can give her something this kid can't."

Marshall raised his eyebrows and shrugged. "Just saying."

"And I'm just saying I have decorum. Rose drops me, I'll just find someone else interested in my supply."

Marshall shook his head. "No one would have you. Not if you turn on Rose. You'd have to move east and work for the Italians. I know you, Abe. You're not going to want to do that."

Abe squinted in thought and relented. "True." He finally took his eyes off Fergus and turned to Marshall "Have you talked to his boys? You're not running for him, are you?"

"I go where Rose tells me to go, but I know where my loyalties are," Marshall said.

Winking, Abe tilted his head to his friend. "Good man."

At the bar, Bradshaw shouted over renewed cheers, "Keep 'em coming!" The group raised their drinks to him and he grinned proudly. His eyes swept over their faces, and he caught sight of Abe and Marshall staring at him from the corner.

Abe spoke to Marshall not hiding the look of contempt on his face, "What a jackass."

Marshall swallowed and lowered his head. "Shit. Here he comes."

Bradshaw approached them and clapped Abe on the shoulder a bit harder than necessary. Abe looked up not taking too kindly to the apparent gesture of friendship. "Marshall! Good seeing you again so soon. How about a drink? Huh?" He looked down at Abe. "How about you, pops! What'll it be?"
Abe shifted in his chair and squared himself to the enthusiastic younger man. "I think I'm alright with what I have, son. Thank you, kindly."

Bradshaw snorted at being rebuffed, "Oh, come on now. Don't be that way. Celebrate with me! I've come into some money, and I want to share the happiness."

Abe gave Bradshaw a dull look and spoke dryly, "You know, you really should be careful flashing that cash around."

Another snort. "Oh, this is a good group, old man. They mean me no harm," Bradshaw said and added loudly for all the room to hear, "Everyone knows there's no crime north of the border!"

The bar cheered in response.

Abe shook his head. "You wouldn't be flashing your cash in, say, an American city, would you? There's dangers in these crowds, too."

Bradshaw considered the other man, a sneer barely hidden behind his wide grin. They stared at one another, sized one another up like gunslingers – like high stakes poker players. Bradshaw leaned closer. "I suppose that depends on who I'm with. Besides, loyalty can be bought."

Abe didn't blink. "Bad seeds in every batch. I'm not saying this to rain on your parade. I'm just saying you need to be careful."

Bradshaw's lip curled, and his smile became a snarl. He eyed Abe suspiciously, unsure. He stuffed the wad of cash back into his jacket. After a beat, Bradshaw smiled. "Who's your friend, Marshall?"

"Abe Calloway," answered for himself, his eyes still locked on Fergus, though he did extend his right hand.

Bradshaw clasped Abe's proffered hand and pumped it twice, holding it tightly, trying to intimidate him with his grip. Abe did not flinch. "Fergus Bradshaw. The pleasure's all mine." He released Abe's hand. "I believe we have a mutual business partner, aside from Marsh here." Bradshaw winked at Marshall, who shifted nervously.

Abe bobbed his head casually. "I don't know what you're talking about."

"Sure you do. You know, come to think of it, I think my Dad spoke of you a time or two."

Abe looked at Fergus pointedly and spoke through his teeth, "No, I'm quite certain I don't know you or your father, Fergus."

Bradshaw laughed and looked around the bar. "Abe! No need to be coy. This whole island knows what you do. What *we* do."

Abe's annoyance was growing. "They do, and they're all smart enough to stay quiet about it. Do you ever wonder why? Cause they ain't stupid."

Bradshaw's eyes narrowed; his jaw clenched.

Abe continued, "I'm sure you're good at what you do, Fergus. Your dad taught you well, and your money speaks to your good work. But you would do well to lower your voice and keep all your inherited success to yourself."

The tension was mounting. Bradshaw stepped closer and glared down at Abe who remained in his chair, leaning back to look up at the larger man. "Enjoy your meal," was all Bradshaw said.

"I will," Abe replied.

Bradshaw stormed back to the bar, raised his arms to get the cheering going again, and Marshall finally exhaled.

"He keeps that up, and if the Mounties don't get him, some blaggards looking for some extra cash will," Abe said.

Marshall shifted anxiously and cleared his throat. "You can only do so much, Abe. You tried to help. The rest is up to him. Now, come on. Enjoy your beer. Forget about the kid."

Abe looked at Fergus a moment longer and returned to his meal. He took up his bitter beer and raised it to his friend. "Well, here's to us old dogs."

Marshall smiled. "Cheers, my friend."

Their glasses clinked, and Abe winced in disgust as he drank. Marshall laughed.

It was later, well into the night, and Fergus Bradshaw made his way along an abandoned logging road. He was drunk and stumbled occasionally. He swayed as he moved down the darkened street singing to himself, "And the ocean waves do roll. And the stormy winds do blow..." As he bellowed the Mermaid tune, Samuel, the young man from the bar, stepped out of the shadows with three friends; the drunkard didn't notice any of them.

"And we poor sailors are skipping at the top... and... um... uh," Bradshaw trailed off, momentarily forgetting the words. He grinned stupidly and went on loudly, "While the landlubbers lie down below, below, below!"

Samuel nodded to his friends with a wicked smirk.

"Then up spoke... uh... Up spoke the..." Bradshaw forgot the words again.

"Then up spoke the captain of our gallant ship, and a fine spoken man was he," Samuel sang in perfect pitch.

Bradshaw staggered around to find Samuel and his posse. He smiled and gave them a wave. "Evening, gentle sirs!"

"Good evening," Samuel nearly bowed, his tone so polite. "Wondering if we could have a minute of your time."

Bradshaw laughed, "Sure. You got a lovely voice, friend. I'll talk wit ya, but it's going to cost you. Time is money, after all!"

The men surrounded the drunk man, Bradshaw looked at them, confused. Hey now, wha's this? What're you doin'? You know who I am?"

Samuel rubbed his chin. "Time *is* money, my friend. And it's going to cost you dearly."

The men closed in on Bradshaw, who was quickly sobering up and realizing what was happening. "Wait! Wait, no!

No! Don't! You can't!" he shouted pointlessly as the four men began to beat him.

The sun rose, and Fergus Bradshaw woke with a grunt in the damp, frosty grass far down the logging road. He held his head, groaning. His face had dried blood along his entire left side. Bruising lined his neck and arms. His jacket was torn. "Ugh," he muttered and staggered to his feet.

He turned a circle, his bloodshot eyes taking in his surroundings. He squinted the rising sun, and a thought hit him. His hand instinctively flew to his chest and patted his pockets frantically. He checked his pants as well. His money was gone.

"Goddammit," he snarled and then added loudly, "Shit!"

He climbed out of the ditch, and a cold fury filled his chest.

CHAPTER NINE

Winter was approaching more each day. The green of the world had faded now. The wind had begun to truly bite and not just after sunset. Abe pulled his jacket around his neck as a particularly strong breeze whipped around the thinning trail to his shack, and he adjusted the sack on his shoulder which contained several ingredients for his work. As he reached the final bend in the path, he was surprised to find his son sitting on the front porch. He smiled despite his gruff exterior and the biting cold, and called out, "Harry! I thought you'd be out working!"

Harry rose from the rocking chair and waved with a grin in return. "I said I would be home for Christmas, didn't I?"

Abe reached his son and gave him a firm squeeze of the shoulder. "Come on, let's get inside. Maybe Chip has a good fire going for us," he joked.

Placing another log in his wood-burning stove, the cabin quickly warmed up. Harry stood bent over the radio tuning it to a station, and "Rhapsody in Blue" began to crackle from the speaker. Harry smiled and stepped back to join his father in the kitchen area. Chip wagged his tail from the bed watching Harry pass and receiving a gentle pat on his furry head.

"Little Curt DeBruin treating you alright at the mill?"

Harry laughed, "Dad, Come on now. Curt's not a kid anymore."

"Ah, " Abe said dismissively, "you'll always be kids to me."

Harry took a seat at the table.

"How is it at the mill? I heard there was a body found last week?"

Harry lowered his eyes. "Yeah," he said. He had been haunted by the body for days now. It had become yet another face in his dreams, and it drew him back to the battlefield. He saw the faces of the men he'd known. Each morning, he awoke with fresh pain from the memories. The shock of seeing someone you know dead never leaves you, he contemplated. The first thing you think is how will you remember them. You'll remember that he could cook, or he could sing, or he was your best friend; and, you'll miss him forever. The crush of grief rolled in behind that. Sometimes you can shove it into the closet for awhile, until you have time to deal with it, and other times, it is forced out by a falling tree and a muddy lump uncovered in the forest.

Abe could see Harry lost in thought, the lingering echoes of war behind his gaze. He hated seeing his son so tortured, and he shut his pantry with a little more force than necessary in order to snap Harry back to the present.

It worked. Harry sniffed and blinked away the ghosts. "We actually finished clearing all the December acres," he said. "Curt has me working the desk now as a reward for helping out so much."

Abe smiled. "Good! That's real good. Good man."

"Not the most fun being stuck inside all day finishing paperwork while everyone leaves for the holiday, but it's nice to feel useful."

Abe pulled up a chair and sat. A new song began its soft melody on the radio. "Ain't Misbehavin'" by Fats Waller:

No one to talk with
All by myself
No one to walk with
But I'm happy on the shelf
Ain't misbehavin'

"If you need a break from the desk job, I know how you could get some fresh air," Abe cocked an eyebrow and his mischievous grin spread over his face.

Harry held up a hand. "We had this conversation, Dad. I'm not joining your business."

"Fishing!" Abe said with a laugh. "I meant we go fishing."

Harry grinned despite himself. "Sure, Dad."

"When's the last time you were out on a stream knee deep in the water snagging kokanee and bull trout or a nice healthy burbot, huh?"

Harry gave his dad a look, not believing his pivot.

Abe shrugged innocently. "You can't blame a man for trying. It's not like I'm getting any younger, and old Chip is pretty useless."

Chip looked at Abe quizzically.

"Sorry, boy. It's the truth. You know it," Abe said.

Abe and Harry sat and listened to the last few bars of "Ain't Misbehavin'." Abe sipped his coffee. "Your Gramma Bess is probably aching to see ya," Abe said. Harry cringed. Abe noticed. He lowered his drink and smirked knowingly. "She don't know you're back on the island, does she?"

Harry's face reddened. "Not exactly," he said sheepishly.

Abe's face grew hard, his tone scolding. "Boy, that is your mother's mother. You best show her the respect she deserves." Abe tried to look stern for a moment, and Harry tensed. Abe's expression melted into a smile and laugh. "Haha. I'd've done the same thing. That woman probably makes the Army look like a day at the beach."

Harry looked up relieved and grinned, still blushing. "I know she means well, but... She's a bit much, isn't she?"

Abe raised his eyebrows. Then he sighed, You're her grandson. She's always going to see you as the little boy who fell out of her tree picking apples."

"God, I remember that. Scrapped my stomach and chest real good on the way down."

"She cut that tree down, you know," Abe said.

"Guess I'm not surprised. Anyone crosses her, she takes them to task."

They sat smiling, listening to the music and drifting back to childhood memories of Bess Kinkle. After a few moments. Abe tightened his lips and pointed a finger. "You really should go see her. She'd probably even let you stay a spell. Helluva lot nicer than this old shack."

"Oh, I don't know about that," Harry said. He bit his lip mustering up some gumption and added, "Do you think I could stay here until Christmas. I mean, here with you?"

Abe studied his son's expression. He saw the sincerity in the boy's face. "Of course," Abe said simply.

Harry looked instantly relieved. "Thank you, Dad."

Abe looked around the small shack. "Not a lot of room, of course, but we can make due."

"I was hoping I could sleep outside even - I mean, I'd build a shack of my own and–"

Abe held up a hand, a thought hitting him. "You can stay on one condition," he said.

Harry blinked at his father.

"You don't put up any fuss over my work out back."

Harry rolled his eyes automatically. "I won't complain, as much as I don't approve."

Abe continued sternly, "And while we're at it, I wouldn't mind you giving me your word that you won't go turning me into the Mounties."

Harry is affronted. He looked at his father, almost hurt by such an accusation. "Dad, you know, as much as I don't like what you do, I would never do that to you. Ever."

"Good," Abe said flatly. "I don't know what I would do without this."

Harry sighed heavily and closed his eyes for a moment. "You don't know what you would do? Dad, you could do anything you want. Hell, you could do nothing. The savings you have, you could sit on your porch until you're old and gray."

"It's not about the money." Abe said.

"Yeah, it's about the thrill," Harry said tersely, an anger rising out of him.

Abe began to rise to the anger as well, his own pride wounded. "No, it's something I'm good at."

The men fell into a tense silence. Harry sighed, shaking his head. He rose from the table and turned to the door, grabbing a fishing pole off the wall.

"Where are you going?" Abe asked with annoyance.

"You're right. It's been too long since I went fishing," Harry replied, his back to his father.

Chip hopped off the bed eager to be outside and trotted to Harry's side. Without another word, they left the shack, shutting the door as they went.

Abe let out a long, heavy sigh.

CHAPTER TEN

The trees swayed back and forth hypnotically. The river tumbled along peacefully. Birds chirped in the treetops, and their melodies mixed with the chunk-chunk of a shovel pounding into dirt. Harry was digging a hole a short distance from his camp. His setup was modest, almost military. He had a hammock, a simple tent with a blanket and a couple of satchels. His bike sat against a tree. Chip lay on the blankets.

Abe walked down the path into the clearing and surveyed it with his hands deep in his pockets. "Nice little camp. Reminds me of our hunting campsites when you were a kid."

Harry looked up. For a moment, he was annoyed to see his father, but quickly, he could see how humble Abe stood, his old head bowed low. Harry stuck the shovel in the dirt and climbed out of his hole brushing off his hands. He peered at his camp, which had taken him only a couple of hours to construct. "We used the same set-up in France. Every now and then, when it was those rare quiet nights, it would feel like those hunting trips."

Abe nodded and strolled closer still glancing around. "Whatchu working on over here?"

Harry gestured to the hole. "Been setting up hunting traps around the area. Might catch a thing or two."

"Hm," Abe replied. He sniffed and cleared his throat. He spoke in what he'd hoped was a casual tone, "Mind if I join you?"

A small smile crossed Harry's lips. "Sure," he said. "I'm trying to scare away the mosquitoes."

Abe sat down on a stump and lit his pipe. "I'm going into town tomorrow. Figured I could pick up anything you need."

"Got everything I need right here. A bed roll, the river, my fishing pole, and the stars above."

Abe smiled and puffed on his pipe. "Well, I'm heading to Jacob's to pick up some copper tubing. Got a leak in the coil I have now. If you think of anything you need, just let me know."

"Thanks, Dad."

Father and son had shared a comfortable moment. Abe rose and looked as though he was going to say more but decided against it. He turned a circle taking in the camp once more, nodding with approval. He began toward the path, and as he went he spoke with his back still to Harry, "Nice little camp. If it gets too cold, you come on inside." He gave a gentle click of his tongue, and Chip hopped up obediently to go after his master.

Harry opened his mouth to say something to his father, but he caught himself as well. A twinge of guilt washed over Harry as he watched Abe go.

Abe walked the dirt path toward town swinging a stick lazily, Chip at his side. The old man's face was tight with deep contemplation. It had been many years since he had to be a father. Harry had left years ago, and if he was being honest with himself, Abe knew that he and Harry had drifted apart when Theodora had passed. She had been the glue between them. She had been the heart and soul and beautiful spirit of their tiny family. Without her, Abe had not known what to do. He had been a dirty little raggamuffin as a child and a wild troublemaker as a teen. Theodora had come from the other side of the island. Her family had been one of the first prominent families of Texada. She had class and wealth. They couldn't have been from more different worlds, and yet when they met, it had been some sort of magic.

The 1st of July, many years ago, Abe had stolen a three-piece suit and a jaunty cap from Captain Bill, the drunk fisherman who Abe had been working for at the docks. Abe strolled into the nice part of the island and had made his way to a gathering of the upper-class. The Zenda family was throwing an Independence Day celebration, and anyone who was anyone was in attendance. Abe blended in the best he was able, drinking their champagne and wine and eating food those people called snacks that were better than any meal he'd seen in years. He mingled with the finer folks, laughing at jokes he didn't understand and doing everything to not pluck watches from pockets.

He snatched cucumber sandwiches by the fistful and shoved them a little too excitedly into his mouth. He guzzled the champagne with enthusiasm, and slipped a biscuit with a spread of pâté into his mouth and immediately spitting it to the ground.

"First time eating pâté?" a light and amused voice asked.

Abe turned, finding a beautiful girl about his age standing in an elegant dark dress with a low cut front and a line of flowers draped along the side. She was shorter than Abe, though her heeled boots gave her several extra centimeters. Her hair was long and pulled up into a stylish pile on her head, though several wisps flew away from the top. She had big, hypnotizing hazel eyes that shimmered with a mysterious secret. And she had a smile of perfectly lined teeth that was so mesmerizing, one couldn't help but think it was meant for only them.

Abe blinked, speechless. A bit of pâté fell from his lips, and he had accidentally smeared some of it on his chin when he'd spit it out.

She walked over to him, took a handkerchief from a small pouch on her waist and wiped the pâté from Abe's chin. "It's awful, isn't it?" she asked.

"Y-yes," Abe managed. He blinked and realized he was gaping at this angel and snapped himself out of it. "I mean, not that I haven't had it before," he affected a more proper tone, or at least what he believed was a tone that made him sound more proper. "I'm used to much better where I'm from."

"Oh really?" the girl raised an eyebrow. "And where would that be?"

"Um," Abe stuttered, "Victoria. The mainland."

"The mainland? Wow," she said with unconvinced surprise. "And you came all the way to our little island to celebrate Independence Day?"

Abe puffed his chest. "Certainly."

She looked the boy over and continued to smile. Abe felt his face growing hot, and he knew he was openingly blushing. She tilted her head, enjoying watching him squirm. Abe bit his lip; his eyes darted about. He leaned close to her. "Please don't say anything," he whispered.

Her smile was genuine. Her interest piqued. She extended her gloved hand to him, palm down. "Theodora," she introduced herself.

Abe swallowed dryly and took her hand. He kissed the top of it and looked up at her as he did. "Abe," he said. "You're very pretty," he said lamely.

"Flatterer," she winked and he blushed even more.

A wave of cheers rippled over the party as the band launched into a grand number and fireworks began to boom overhead, but neither Abe nor Theodora looked up at them. They stared at one another for a long time, and that was it. Abe was in love. The moment they touched, the moment they truly looked at one another, the splashes of red and blue and green washing over her skin, lighting her eyes with fire–her hazel eyes drawing him in; that smile and the tiny freckle under her right eye – everything she was, Abe wanted in his life.

He stood up fully and licked his lips. "Would you like to dance?" he asked.

"I would," she replied happily.

Under the bursts of color, surrounded by the cheering world Abe had no place within, the young couple danced. Abe's life truly began then and there. She ignited a fire within him he had not known existed. She challenged him to be a better man, and he wanted to be. That was her power; that was what she did to people. She brought out the best in a man. Her heart was so big, and that kindness and serenity made her perfect in Abe's eyes, though she would protest such a moniker whenever he would say it.

Life was joyous with Theodora, despite what her mother and father thought of that dastardly Abe Calloway from the wrong side of the island. Days at the beach meant more to Abe with her; nights under the stars meant everything. They danced and laughed and made love. They married and brought Harry into the world. Motherhood suited her far better than fatherhood suited Abe. She guided their little Harry through the world like a shepherd, educating him and molding him into the fine man he would become without her.

And when she grew sick, when the darkness of the world clawed its way into her perfection, Abe knew that he would be lost without her. He knew that he and Harry could never survive without her, and he had been right.

When he held her for the last time, her breath growing weaker, she spoke so quietly, "Abe, my love."

"I'm here," he whimpered, his fortitude failing him. "I'm here."

She was on her bed. Harry, barely ten-years-old was curled into a ball beside her fast and deeply asleep. Abe sat on the bed on her other side holding her hand in his.

"Remember the night we met?" she whispered.

"Of course."

"You were so handsome in that terrible suit," she said, and her beautiful smile found its way onto her pale face.

Abe held her face in his hands. "And you were an angel."

"And we danced," she said weakly, though the smile remained.

"We did."

"Will you," her voice was trailing away, "dance with me again?"

"Forever," he said, choking back tears.

"Good," she said. The word was barely audible now. Her eyes closed.

Abe sniffed, tears coming down his cheek.

Her voice rose and she kissed little Harry on the top of his sleeping head. "Be strong for him."

"I'll try," Abe said.

She lay quietly then, her breath slower and slower. He lay beside her and held her so closely. The tears streamed from his eyes, and his lip trembled.

"Abe?"

"I'm here."

"Thank you."

He shook his head and spoke through his sniffles, "No, thank you, Theo. Thank you for being my purpose in this whole damn world."

She smiled. It was a perfect smile. "Flatterer," she whispered.

Before the sun rose, Theodora Calloway had passed away, and everything Abe was and everything he'd ever wanted to be died with her. He was lost. He was scared. He was confused. He tried his best to be a father to Harry, but without his angel to shepherd him, he slipped back to the life he knew before he'd met her. He moved them back to his side of the island. He started running with his old crowd. He lost his way, and with it, the gap between himself and his son grew with every year that passed. Abe didn't know what his purpose was anymore. How could he help Harry find his?

Abe swung the stick in his hand and kicked a pebble, which Chip chased after playfully - albeit slowly. The sun shone down through the trees on the path, and as the remaining leaves on branches flitted about, a display of shadows and light played like fireworks at his feet.

"I hope he finds his way," Abe muttered aloud to Chip. "Every man needs his purpose, and that boy deserves a noble one. Something that makes him feel happy and whole. Do something he loves, like you and me, pal."

Chip looked up at Abe, and Abe went on as though they were having a full conversation, "Well, we all have to make a living somehow. Even if the Mounties and the Americans frown on it, I'm just making people happy, right?"

He looked down at Chip, expecting an answer, nodding, "Of course I'm right. Keeps me fed, keeps you fed, everyone's happy."

Abe paused his stroll and tucked the stick under his arm. He reached into his pocket and pulled out a list written in his scraggly handwriting. "Let's see," he said. "Could use some molasses for this next batch. I wonder if Jimmy Holmes wants to make a trade."

Chip eyed the stick in anticipation. Abe gave a sidelong glance to the pup and smirked. "You see the stick, boy?" He held out the branch. "See it?"

Chip barked happily.

"Go get it!" Abe chucked the stick as hard as he could into the woods. Chip ran off after it. Abe chuckled and continued down the path. "Still just a pup ain'tcha?" he asked the wind.

He looked up through the leaves at the glimmer of sun. Somewhere out there in the beyond, he prayed that Theodora was looking down on him. Maybe she'd brought Harry back to the island. Maybe she had protected him through the Great War and returned him to Abe. Maybe he would finally be the father Harry needed, or at the very least, a friend. He allowed himself a soft grin at the thought of that possibility. Was that Theo's plan? He wondered, and then he chuckled knowingly. "Or is Harry here to show me the error of my ways?" he asked his wife.

"Afternoon, Calloway," a deep rumble of a voice snapped Abe back to the moment. He stopped walking. Standing in the path just ahead of Abe was a bruiser of a man with greasy, slicked back hair and a brute of a man with the look of a Neanderthal. It was Earl Martin and RJ Johnson, Fergus Bradshaw's men.

Abe frowned and spoke cautiously, "Earl; RJ. Something I can do for you two?"

Earl chewed a toothpick and had his hands in his pockets. "Word has it you had some of your boys jump Fergus Bradshaw the other night."

Abe laughed, "My boys? I think you've got the wrong guy, fellas." He shook his head and proceeded to continue his walk.

Earl stuck out a hand and touched Abe's chest, stopping him. "No, no I don't think we do. See, Fergus says you was acting pretty tough at the pub. Trying to piss on your territory 'cause you didn't like him showing off. Then someone went ahead and put the beating on him real bad."

Abe looked down at his chest where Earl had touched him. He looked up and asked genuinely, "Is he okay?"

"No, he ain't!" Earl snapped. "And he ain't too happy with you either! You or that posse you sent at him."

Abe exhaled, "Posse? I don't have a posse; I work alone." He thought for a moment. "Well, mostly alone." He turned and gave a whistle over his shoulder.

Chip raced out of the woods with the stick in his mouth and abruptly halted at the sight before him on the road. He dropped the stick and growled at the two men.

RJ sneered and grunted to his cohort, "Earl, he's got a dog."

"I can see that," Earl said snidely. "Take care of it."

RJ made a move, and Abe stepped in the massive man's path. "You leave my dog alone!"

Everything happened fast. Earl grabbed Abe by the front of his shirt and threw him to the ground. The old man fell hard, not ready for the sudden attack, his bag flying off his shoulder and his hand landing on Chip's stick. RJ kicked Chip across the torso, causing the poor dog to yelp and roll through the dirt. He lumbered over to the fallen animal and planted a foot on his neck, pinning Chip to the ground.

Abe snatched up the stick and clubbed Earl across the side of his face. Earl reeled about and punched Abe in the head, dazing him.

"Keep that thing back!" Earl shouted to RJ and clambered to his feet. He stomped over to the old man and yanked Abe to his knees, punching him with a tight, closed fist in the face. Abe fell back, shook off the blow, and kicked Earl as hard as he could in the knee. As his knee popped loudly, Earl screamed in agony. Enraged, he tackled Abe and began punching him in the kidneys. Abe gasped for breath, unable to protect himself from the swift attack.

Earl rose, breathing heavily. He slicked back his loose hair and glared at Abe who was writhing in the dirt. Earl bent down and picked up the stick. He limped over to his fallen opponent and towered over him.

RJ looked at Earl, shaking his head. "Easy," he muttered. "Fergus said to send him a message, not kill him."

Earl glared down at Abe, an ugly sneer on his face with a trickle of blood at the corner of his mouth. He raised the stick and swung it down into Abe's stomach, hard, taking the last wind out of the old man.

Bending over Abe, Earl hissed into the old man's ear, "You just started a war, old man. Bradshaw is taking over Texada. Your days as a moonshiner on this island are numbered. Next time we see ya, we'll kill ya."

Earl rose and spit on Abe before he turned back to RJ, "Okay, Let his dog go. Stupid mutt's no threat anyway."

RJ released the dog and scooped up Abe's bag of supplies. Without another word, he and Earl walk away, Earl with a limp thanks to a no-doubt shattered knee.

Chip barked weakly at the two men but remains at Abe's side protectively. Abe lay staring up at the canopy of leaves in pain. "Good boy, Chip," he said weakly and groaned from the pain all over his body. He stared at the flickering light through the leaves and tried to imagine Theodora's tender embrace. "Shit," he coughed.

CHAPTER ELEVEN

Harry sat beside a fire eating a modest meal and humming peacefully to himself when Abe came limping out of the forest. Harry glimpsed him and smiled. "I was wondering when you–" he nearly dropped his tin of beans and shot up to a standing position. "Dad!"

Abe stepped into the light. He was covered in bruises and dried blood.

"What happened to you? Here, sit down! Good Lord. What happened?" Harry babbled and eased his father down onto the stump.

Abe held his aching head. "Ah, some assholes. Some of Bradshaw's men. They snuck up on me in the woods and attacked us."

Chip came limping out up beside them and laid by the fire. The poor dog's ego was as bruised as his body.

"Bradshaw? Who the hell is Bradshaw?" Harry demanded as he examined Abe's wounds.

Abe pushed Harry's hands away. "He's some new hotshot moonshiner. Thinks he's gonna take over Texada."

"But what did you do to him? Why did he do this? Are you – Did you do something?"

"No, no nothing. Nothing like that. Idiot thinks I sent some local guys to rob him a couple nights ago."

Harry's eyes narrowed. "You didn't, did you?"

Abe scoffed humorlessly and gestured to his bruised. "After this? Kinda wish I'd beat his ass myself." He registered the shock on his son's face and added, "But no, I didn't do nothing."

Harry rose and stepped back from his father. He clenched his jaw tightly. His heart was hammering inside his chest. "Who is this guy?"

"I told you, he's nobody," Abe grunted and adjusted his body on the stump.

"Well, this won't stand," Harry said firmly. "A man can't just beat another man for no reason. Some gangster trying to push you around for something you didn't even do? No." He began to pace. "You're well-connected around here, Dad. I'm sure you know some people who could, I don't know, get rid of this guy."

Abe shrugged. "Well, yes, but you can't think I'd retaliate or–or–or plot something. That's not how I do things. I just make booze, and I let my booze do the talking for me. For chrissake, I'm a bootlegger, not some gangster."

"Fine," Harry said. He held up his hands and stopped pacing. He moved to one of his satchels and fetched some bandages. He returned to the stump and gently applied field dressings. His training returned to him easily. He was back in the trenches. He cleaned his father up, but the younger man's blood was pumping hard. "Let me fix your bootlegging ass up," he grunted.

As he dressed the wounds, Harry went on, "I don't know what you have to do to keep yourself safe, and I don't want to know. But I don't want you getting yourself killed."

"Hare, I'll be fine."

"That should help," Harry said putting the last bandage on his father's neck. "Come on, you should lay down."

"It's fine–" Abe started but stopped protesting as he winced.

Harry helped his dad to his feet and moved him to the tent. He set him as gently as he was able on the bedroll, and Abe patted his son's arm thankfully. Harry took a blanket and pulled it over Abe. "Just relax, okay?"

"Alright," Abe sighed, the fight out of him and sleep taking over.

Harry stepped back from the tent and put his hands on his hips. He looked over at Chip. The poor dog got up slowly and moved to lay beside Abe.

With his eyes closed, Abe patted Chip's head. "Nice to know he really cares, eh, boy?" Abe said to Chip.

"I heard that," Harry said from the fire as he cleaned up his discarded meal.

Abe grinned in spite of the pain.

Harry had calmed. He pulled up an apple box and sat beside his father. "So tell me about this Bradshaw guy." He took out a canteen and dribbled water on a rag.

"There's not a lot more to say. He's young, he's loud, he's overconfident. Boss Rose's newest supplier, apparently."

"Boss Rose?" Harry screwed up his face at the name.

"Prohibition Rose. She's runs a huge chunk of the booze trade in the Northwest. Real piece of work."

Harry applied the wet cloth to Abe's head, cleaning up some of the blood.

"Oh, that's better already. Thank you," Abe said gratefully.

"A woman?" Harry asked.

"Yep," Abe said. "She's been running things since the start."

"Really?" Harry was surprised. "She hasn't been busted yet?"

Abe raised his brow, a look of admiration on his face. "You find the right clients, you never have to worry about that."

Harry looked down at his dad suspiciously. "You know, it kinda sounds like you like this woman."

Abe chuckled lightly, "Sure, I respect her. She's a good business woman."

"And?"

"And what?"

"Is she attractive?"

Abe looked at his son. "Now, I don't know what that has to do with anything." His face reddened ever-so-slightly on his cheeks.

Harry smirked at his dad. He looked over at Chip. "She's attractive, isn't she?"

Abe's lips turned down in a deep frown. "Harrison Otis Oliver Calloway."

Harry attempted to keep a straight face and continued to talk to Chip. "He's using the full name. I'm in trouble."

Chip wagged his tail.

Abe rolled his eyes. "Besides, I wouldn't risk it. What I do comes with risk and with a price and a healthy case of paranoia."

Harry gestured to the bruises. "I can see that, Dad. Thank you."

Abe grimaced. He could see the worry on his sons face. He could see how hard this all was on him. "I'm sorry," Abe said in a tone not unlike a child speaking to their parent.

Harry sighed, "You're lucky they didn't kill you.

They looked at one another, and Abe's cheeks flushed again, embarrassed by his condition.

Harry added with a wry smirk, "I mean, where would that leave Chip?"

Abe chuckled and winced from his bruised ribs.

Harry offered him the canteen, and Abe took a long sip. He handed it back and looked at his boy. "You're a strong young man. Stubborn as a mule sometimes, thanks to me, but you're smart."

"Thanks," Harry said.

Abe reached out and touched his son's hand. "You know, you'd make it on your own if you needed to. You're a soldier, Harry."

Harry shook his head. "I'm not about to lose you over some booze feud."

Abe smiled softly. "I had no idea you cared."

Harry exhaled, "Of course I do. I wouldn't be out here patching you up if I didn't. I wouldn't be out here at all."

The men fell into a slightly more comfortable silence as Harry put away the bandages. He returned to the tent and sat again. He looked at his dad. "Do you remember that Christmas when I was nine? When I tried to surprise you and mom?"

Abe smiled sadly, though there was a fondness in the memory. "You thought you would surprise us early in the morning with a nice, warm house."

"And I tried to start the stove without opening the flue."

"And the smoke pouring into the house convinced you that Santa Claus somehow got stuck in our stovepipe." Abe's snicker turned into full laughter. He held his side in pain. "Haha-oh-ouch-haha!"

"Sorry," Harry said through his own chuckling.

"It's okay, It's okay." Abe wiped a tear from the corner of his eye.

"It was a perfectly logical fear at the time," Harry said.

"You came running into the bedroom," Abe put on a childlike voice "Mama, Dad! The house is smoky and Santa's stuck! Help me before I cook him!"

Harry was laughing now, the first time he has done so in a long while.

"Thank God none of the neighbors saw the smoke," Abe said.

"We did manage to save Santa though," Harry pointed. "Didn't hear about a single kid who didn't get a gift that year."

"That's right. Our little hero," Abe declared.

The two of them laughed and slowly relaxed. They looked up at the stars together and sat in each other's company, father and son.

"You should rest," Harry instructed. "No moonshining tomorrow. That's an order."

Abe offered a salute. "Sir, yes, sir." He groaned a bit from the movement. "I'm in no shape to work anyway. A day of rest is a good idea."

"Good," Harry said.

"You sure you don't mind if we sleep out here with you tonight?"

Harry smiled. "I'd like that. It'll be just like our old hunting trips."

Abe nodded absentmindedly. Fatigue finally overtaking him. He lay back and closed his eyes. Chip was already asleep by his side.

Harry watched his father's breathing slow and become a soft snore. He moved to the fire and warmed his hands. He looked up at the stars and stared at them until his eyes began to droop.

CHAPTER TWELVE

Three days had passed, and though Abe was still banged up, his wounds had healed a bit. Humming to himself, a winter scarf wrapped around his neck, he used a stick as a cane and circled his still working on a new batch of booze. Chip trotted around his legs, tail wagging.

"What do ya think, Chip? Think this coil'll hold?" Abe muttered as he fiddled with the new part in his contraption.

Chip barked.

Abe turned his attention to the condenser briefly. He tested the pipe to see if it was leaking and was satisfied that it appeared to be holding up just fine. He patted the side of the still like an old friend. "Good girl," he said with a smile. He pulled out a spoon and tapped it on the side of his leg thoughtfully.

Abe stepped back and Chip circled around him expectantly. He sniffed the spoon and recoiled knowing the scent all too well. Abe chuckled, "Guess that means three days flat on my ass and I haven't lost my touch."

From the house, Harry limped down the trail in a heavy jacket and stopped at the edge of the clearing. He scowled and adjusted his glasses. "I thought three days of rest would put some sense in you."

Abe flinched, startled by the sudden appearance of his son. A hint of paranoia had come over the old man since his beating. He cleared his throat and leaned on his walking stick. "Hell, I oughta put a bell on you, son."

Harry walked to his father and gestured to Abe's wounded leg. "You really think you should be out of bed and back here brewing, Dad?"

"No rest for the wicked," Abe grinned. "And it's moonshining, you teetotaler." He shuffled around the still. "You know, you really oughta go see your grandma Bess. She's going to have my hide if I keep hogging you all to myself."

"I'll go see her eventually." Harry strolled over to the still and looked it over curiously. The clicks and clanks created a hypnotic rhythm. The turning gears and moving liquid popped and hissed. "You built this all on your own, huh?"

Abe puffed his chest proudly. "Built it. Maintain it. Appreciate it."

"Pretty clever use of skill," Harry said.

Abe eyed Harry, suspicious of his flattery. "What're you ramping up to?"

Harry feigned ignorance, "What? I'm not," but his words are cut off by the knowing look from his father. Harry balked. No sense in beating around the bush. "You could put your skills with machines to better use."

Abe groaned with exasperation, "Here we go. You can't just leave me alone, can you?"

Harry shook his head and put his hands on his hips. "I gotta try at least one more time."

Abe walked over to a barrel and took a seat, grunting from stiffness. Chip came to his side, and Abe scratched the pooch behind the ear. "Alright," Abe said with another heavy sigh. "Go ahead."

Harry began to pace, his limp not so bad today. He gesticulated like an attorney making his case before the court. "It's illegal, Dad. You could get arrested. You could be killed. You could do so many other things. Your mechanical prowess is clear by the look of this," Harry looked at the still, "extraordinary contraption. This sort of ability could be put to use for the community all over the island. Boats and cars always need sharp minds and able hands."

"I am serving the community," Abe said plainly.

"Not like this," Harry lamented. "Your time could be so much better spent."

"God's sake, who cares what I do with my time? I'm a businessman supplying goods for a legitimate organization in Portland, as I am free to do in this country. Been doing it for years and hardly a word of trouble or opposition until you came home."

Harry raised his hands. "This isn't a fight. I'm not here to argue. I just," Harry looked at his dad trying to get through to him. "I just needed to say all this one more time without us falling into silence or storming off."

"Only one who storms off is you," Abe grunted.

"I'm not here to fight," Harry repeated.

Abe glowered, "Feels like you want to, boy."

"I'm not a boy anymore, Dad," Harry said sourly. I've seen the world."

"Here we go," Abe said and rolled his eyes. "Man of the world," he mocked.

Harry raised his voice. "I know things! And I know this, that still is not how a man should live."

"Why in the holy hell does this mean so much to you!" Abe shouted. "It's just booze! It's just drinking! It's how people escape and relax and get through their goddamn days!"

Harry's face flushed. They stared at each other, another argument about to unfold. Abe opened his mouth to retort further—

POW! The new coil snapped off the still and flew from the innards of the contraption like a bullet. Harry ducked as steam erupted from the break like a hot spring geyser. The entire still began to quake violently.

"Damn!" Abe leapt into action.

Harry moved to help. "What can I do?" he shouted over the commotion.

"Turn that valve!"

"Okay! I got it!" Harry raced to follow his father's instructions.

The giant machine began to squeal. Abe gripped the side of it and twisted knobs while shouting to Harry, "Turn it all the way to the right! Yeah, turn it all the way around."

"Okay!"

"Yes! There! Okay, let's go!"

Abe grabbed a wrench and jammed the coil back in place. He twisted it with all his might. As he did, the vibrations began to subside, and finally, the breach was contained, and the machine returned to its proper operation.

The two men stepped back, both wary and waiting for another break. After several pounding heartbeats, they began to relax. Abe chuckled and patted his boy's arm. "It's done," he said breathlessly. "Well done, boy. That was some swift action."

"Thanks," Harry grinned and nodded, catching his own breath.

"That's that military training in ya, isn't it?" Abe said.

Harry thought about that for a moment. It was true. His calm under pressure had been beaten into him. His instincts for action were as sharp as they'd been in Europe.

Abe walked back over to the barrel and plopped down, winded. They sat and listened to the machine chug for a minute. The still was once more beating and clunking its rhythmic song.

Harry watched the still, his heart and breath settling, though his mind continued to twist around the realization of how much of a soldier he still was. The machine had gone off like a mortar, and he hadn't hesitated for an instant. He stepped back and sat on the barrel next to Abe. He lowered his gaze and began to speak, not sure where his words were coming from. "I've seen a lot of things I wish I hadn't."

Abe looked at his son, surprised by the sudden words.

Harry went on, his eyes lost in the middle distance. "Men fighting. Men dying. And after living through things like that, there are only so many options for a man to just forget it all, even if only for a night." His eyes were glazed over but his words were clear over the din of the still. "Some of the men I fought beside used women. Some of them did it with more fighting. Some of them just couldn't take it anymore, and killed themselves. And me," he trailed off, his voice barely a whisper. "I drank."

Abe sat up. He listened to his son with silent reverence. The sadness of Harry's words filled Abe, and he listened to his son open up with sorrow.

"Every time we made it back from the battlefield, we'd all go out and drink ourselves stupid. To feel anything else but what we were feeling. We left so many men behind." Harry squeezed his bad knee. "When I had booze in me, I was numb. I could go on. I could fight another day like a good soldier."

Harry fell silent for a thoughtful moment. Abe let him take his time.

"Christmas Eve, last year, I went to a pub in London with two of my friends. Two fellow soldiers. We'd been fighting together since the start. We were going to celebrate. The season, or maybe just being alive." He smiled at the memory. It was a sad smile. He went on.

"We were ready to whip up a frenzy, have a grand time, talk to the local girls. Have a ball while there was a ball to be had." In his memories, the music of the night began to play. The soft, swinging jazz of a live band. The squeals of the beautiful girls and the clink of pints. He could sense it all again.

"Eat, drink, and be merry, for tomorrow we could be dead, right?" He laughed sardonically.

Abe smiled slightly at the words.

Harry's smile faded. "We ran into an officer we hadn't seen in months. A corporal who'd been discharged after he lost his arm. He was there, singing and drinking and buying rounds. And I looked at him. Looked at this ruined man laughing and drinking himself stupid, and I just wasn't in the mood anymore." Harry's face grew somber. "I didn't even know why I'd gone out in the first place anymore. It was Christmas, but to me, it was just another night before another damn day."

Harry shifted. He squeezed his leg tighter. Abe sat in silence still.

"I felt worse and worse as the night went on, so I just left. Stumbled my way back to the base. Don't even remember how I got there." He paused. A glimmer of tears formed at the corner of his eyes.

Abe bit his cheek. He wanted to reach out to his son, but he didn't want to stop him from opening up either.

Harry composed himself. "In the morning, I waited. For hours on end, I waited for my friends to come back to the barracks, and they never did. They were killed that night, Dad."

Abe drew a breath.

Harry stared forward. "After I'd left, they'd gotten so drunk–so rowdy that they'd gotten in a brawl with some local toughs. I don't even know what it was about, but after one got glassed and bled to death just outside the pub, the other stumbled into the street and was hit by a cart. Run over by a horse."

Abe bowed his head slightly, respectfully.

Harry went on. This was the first time he had ever said any of this out loud. His eyes were filled with unshod tears from repressing all of this. "I don't blame the booze. I don't. The booze actually saved my life, didn't it? But I couldn't numb myself to it all anymore. It's bad enough they died young and away from home. It was no hero's death. It was foolish. It was a senseless act that wouldn't have happened if they just had their wits about them, or if I'd have had mine. But no, I don't blame the booze."

He finally blinked, and a single tear fell to the dirt at his feet. He looked at Abe with a hard, stony face. "But I don't want to sit here and pretend I don't hate what it does to people. Makes 'em fools. Makes 'em greedy. Turns men into devils. Makes 'em forget who they are. Makes 'em violent. And I don't want to see anyone else die when I can do something about it."

He looked off into the trees, the sun sparkled through the thinning tree branches. "I left the Army because of that fact. I lived in the middle of nowhere in Manitoba all these years because of that. And I came back home because of it." He looked at Abe once more. "I don't want you to die, Dad. Not because of this."

Silence. He had said everything he'd wanted to. More than he probably thought he ever would. Abe shifted and faced his son fully. He looked at Harry as though seeing him for the first time. This man, beaten by war and death. This man who truly had seen things and was a man of the world.

Abe spoke gently, humble, "I'm sorry you went through all that, Harry. Sorry for your friends."

"The Army told the families they died heroically in battle," Harry said with a humorless laugh. He shook his head. "They can never know the truth. Never."

Abe sighed deeply, shaking his head mournfully. He touched the ring on his left hand with his thumb. "I'm sorry about that, Harry. Losing people who are close to you will cause a lot of hurt."

"Yeah?" Harry asked almost childlike. "Does it get any easier?"

Abe rubbed dirt from his wedding band. His heart was heavy. "Later on in life."

Harry nodded, thankful to hear it.

Abe put a warm hand on Harry's shoulder. "I'm here for you, Harry. I know you and I don't see eye to eye on a lot of things, most of all my business, but I just need you to know that I love you."

Harry met his father's gaze. "Just make me a promise."

"Yeah?"

"Think about hanging up your hat and retiring from all this."

"Harry–"

"Just think about it."

Abe opened his mouth to speak, but he closed it, trying to gather his thoughts. He rubbed his neck, still sore from his beating. He thought of Bradshaw and his goons. He thought of Rose and Marshall. He thought of his beloved Theodora, and he looked into his son's face and saw the little boy behind the eyes of a man who's seen so much. Abe shrugged with one shoulder.

"I suppose maybe there wouldn't be any harm in laying low for a spell. Wait for this Bradshaw drifter to drift back to wherever he came from."

A small smile crossed Harry's face. "Exactly," he said.

Abe held out his right hand to Harry as if to shake on it. "I'm sorry, Harry. I didn't mean to put you through this much trouble."

Harry took his father's hand and pulled Abe in for a hug. It is a tender moment. "I love you."

"I know," Abe grunted manly.

"Even if you're a stubborn ass," Harry added.

"Takes one to know one, son."

The two men share a laugh. Chip nudged Abe's hand. Abe looked at the old pup and stuck out his lip thoughtfully. "Oh, it won't be so bad, Chip. No pressure. No deadlines. No trying to dodge the Mounties or border police. Just a man and his dog, living within the confines of the law."

Chip barked and wagged his tail.

"Suppose that means you're on board, eh?" Abe said.

Chip barked again. The still chugged and grinded on. The wind blew, a little colder now, but the sun shone warmly on the family.

CHAPTER THIRTEEN

A gentle dusting of frost in the now barren treetops was met by gossamer flakes that melted just as soon as they kissed the ground. As the sun made its way over the hills and greeted the island with morning rays, fishermen made their way out onto the rocky beach, including Abe and, naturally, Chip.

Abe found a secluded spot and cast out his line watching it splash into the water and send ripples in halos over the calm surface. He stared at his line placidly, content with the world and life. He settled onto a small folding chair he'd brought with him and turned to his dog. "How they biting over there?"

Chip looked around, tongue hanging out, happy to be wherever he was.

"You've got it all figured out, eh, dog? Not a care in the world except supper time."

Abe reeled in his line slightly. It jerked. "Oh, hang on! We got one!" He set the hook and and started to reel it in.

Chip perked up, expectant. He watched with his tail wagging furiously as his master battled the catch. He barked encouragement, and Abe grit his teeth. Down the beach, a pair of other fishermen watched with smiles.

By midafternoon, Abe and Chip were walking back to the shack with an admirable collection of fish trapped in a net slung across the old man's back. Chip trotted beside him with his furry head held high, certain he was the reason they'd done so well. As they came over the last rise of the thin road to the cabin, Abe spotted a slumped figure rocking in his chair on the porch with his hat dipped over his eyes.

Abe gave a sharp whistle, and Marshall lifted the brim of his hat. Abe waved and closed the final distance between them.

Marshall stepped off the porch to meet Abe on the path and stopped short. His eyes went wide seeing the cuts and purple-yellow bruises on Abe's neck and face. "Holy crow! What happened to you?" He gasped.

Abe grimaced. "Bradshaw."

Marshall was shocked. "Fergus Bradshaw did this to you?" he gaped.

"Na, a couple of his friends. They thought I sent a posse after him."

Abe pulled the net off his shoulder and set it down on the porch. He rubbed his sore back. "Do you mind helping me out here? Shoulder is still healing."

Marshall nodded and grabbed the net full of fish. "Oh sure, of course," Marshall said as the two men walked into the shack. "Are you alright?"

Abe pulled off his jacket and moved to the stove to toss another log into it, the last embers of the morning's fire dwindling. "I'm no worse for wear; I'll be good as new in, oh, a week, maybe two."

"Goddamn, Abe," Marshall exhaled. "Harry been around?"

"He has. Made camp just down a ways. He's still working at the mill. Probably for the best. He sees you, and he might get a little disappointed in me. He's not too fond of anything involving the business. Been a fine point of contention since he came back."

"Sorry to hear that," Marshall said. "Where do you want these?" he asked, meaning the fish.

"Just leave them in the sink for now. I'll clean them later."

Marshall obliged and set them in the basin on the counter. "I'll throw some ice on them." He opened the small ice box against the wall and pulled out a handful of ice, which he tossed on the fish.

Abe groaned as he took a seat on his bed. Chip curled up at his feet.

Marshall peeked toward the backdoor and then turned to his friend. "So I take it you don't have anything for me yet, eh?"

Abe shook his head. "I made a promise. I said I would rest and lay low, so I'm resting and laying low."

"Now why would you go and do a thing like that? The boss is going to notice. She's not going to be happy. You remember Rodrigu—"

"Yesah, yeah, I remember Rodriguez, and if you compare me to that cheating shyster again, I've a mind to toss you in the lake."

Marshall put up his hands. "Alright; I'm just saying, you don't wanna cross Boss Rose."

Abe lifted his shoulders and let them fall. "If she saw what kind of shape I was in, I hardly think she would hold it against me."

Marshall dragged a chair to the middle of the room and faced Abe as he sat. He removed his flask from his pocket and took a nip. "Well, still," he said.

Abe leaned back on his bed and tipped his hat over his eyes, much like Marshall had been doing on the porch. "It's not much, but you're welcome to take what's at the still. Just know it might be the last little bit for a few weeks."

Marshall twisted his mouth anxiously and rubbed the back of his neck. "Are you sure about this?"

"Yep," Abe said from behind his hat. "Trying to do right by Harry."

"And Boss Rose?"

Abe used the tip of his finger and raised the brim of his hat just enough to show one eye and look at Marshall, unimpressed and slightly annoyed. "Look, just because you are scared of that little woman doesn't mean I am. I respect her, don't get me wrong, but I have a legitimate reason to quiet down on the bootlegging for a spell." He lowered the brim back over his face. "If she doesn't understand that, I'll eat my hat. I'll send her my last load, move off of Texada, and take my business elsewhere."

Marshall narrowed his eyes. "You're bluffing, Abe Calloway."

Abe chuckled quietly to himself and replied confidently. "I know her better than you think I do. She'll wait."

Marshall made his lips a line and widened his eyes. "Okay," he extended the word. "Whatever you say."

Abe sat up and tossed his hat onto Chip's head. "She's a good, faithful customer. She's harsh, sure, but she is fair. Tell her about Bradshaw. Tell her I'm laid up in bed eating apple sauce through a straw. Now, can I depend on you to tell her all that?"

Marshall shifted anxiously. "Yeah, of course. I'm just worried."

Abe leaned forward and narrowed his eyes. The wry grin that sat perpetually at the edges of his mouth was sneaking out for Marshall to see. "Whose booze do the people really want, Marshall? Mine or Bradshaw's?"

Marshal exhaled through his nose. "Alright! I get the message. You're an ornery old son of a gun, you know that?"

Abe grinned widely. "That's the way I am. That's the way I'm always going to be. Now, how about we whip up some of those fish?"

Chip's ear perked up and shifted the hat off his head.

Outside the window, the stars began to come out, and flakes of snow flitted through the sky.

CHAPTER FOURTEEN

Snow fell lightly on the harbor as the Malahat bobbed into the docks. The late afternoon sun was attempting to push through the cloud cover, creating a glow in the western horizon. As the men of the fishing ship pushed their cargo from below deck to the dock, Marshall hopped off the gangplank and disembarked to meet Rose, Jake just behind her, as always.

Rose eyed the contents coming from the Malahat and hummed a low tone. She moved closer to inspect the half dozen barrels, a much smaller load than usual. She kept her hands in her pockets and spoke to Marshall without looking at him. "Kegs from Abe Calloway?"

Marshall shifted nervously. "Yes, ma'am. I'm afraid so."

Rose walked to a barrel stacked atop another and placed a gloved hand on it. She rolled her fingers over it a moment and then tilted a glance to Jake. Jake obediently walked to her, tapped the keg, produced a small glass from his jacket and poured a single shot for Boss Rose. She took it and downed it easily. She winced as it burned her throat. She exhaled and shook her head. The tone of her voice was level, "It's good, but there's not enough of it. This isn't like Calloway. What happened?"

Marshall cleared his throat nervously. Rose stared at him expectantly, only making him more nervous. "Well, um,

Abraham–I mean Abe. He got jumped a couple weeks ago. He's hurt pretty bad."

Rose raised her brow. "Jumped? Who would jump an old man like Abe?"

"He said it was a couple of Bradshaw's boys, Boss."

Rose's surprise doubled. "Bradshaw?"

Marshall shuffled his feet like a schoolboy before his teacher. "Bradshaw got mugged and he thought Abe was responsible, so he–I mean Fergus– he decided to retaliate."

Rose narrowed her eyes and stepped closer to Marshall. She removed her glove from one hand and touched Marshall's cheek. It was a seemingly warm gesture, but Marshall stiffened. "Is that the truth, Marshall?"

"Of course!" Marshall replied instantly and winced at himself for being so forceful to the boss. "I mean," he said with a humble lowered gaze, "es, Boss."

Rose lightly slapped the side of Marshall's face and looked to Jake. Her bodyguard's face was tight, like a spring loaded trap waiting to be tripped. Rose tilted her head in a questioning movement.

"You don't think Calloway did it, do you, Boss?" Jake asked.

Marshall flinched again, not used to hearing Jake's gravelly voice. It sound like stones rubbing against one another.

Rose shook her head assuredly. "Abe's an honest man–as honest as a moonshiner can get. He wouldn't take anything that wasn't rightfully his, and I don't think anyone would take it in his name. Probably some local ruffians making trouble. Correct, Marshall?"

Marshall nodded quickly. "Y-yes, Boss."

Rose reached out and squeezed Marshall's shoulder. Another seemingly kind gesture that once more made Marshall tense. "You tell Abe the next time Bradshaw gives him the business, I'm sending Jake. I will not have any in-fighting in my racket. Is that understood?"

Marshall nodded vigorously. This woman clearly intimidated him. She smiled at how obviously that was written on the man's face. "Don't just nod. I want to hear you say it," Rose said through her cold smile.

"Y-yes, ma'am. If Bradshaw gives Abe anymore trouble, you'll send J-Jake."

Rose patted Marshall's arm one final time. "Good man. I admire your loyalty." She stepped closer–too close. He kept looking forward like a soldier. She looked up at him; he was a full head taller than she was, and her nose almost touched Marshall's chin. "I appreciate loyalty. You wouldn't hold out on me, would you?"

Marshall swallowed dryly and shook his head adamantly. "Boss, I wouldn't dream of double-crossing you."

Rose smiled. "Naturally. You can't be too careful though. You're a good runner. I appreciate your loyalty to both myself and to Calloway. I intend to repay a favor with a favor. You can stay with the girls tonight if you want to. It's on me."

Marshall lowered his gaze with wide, surprised eyes. "Really?"

Rose smiled more warmly now and stepped back. She gestured to the warehouse. "Of course."

"Wow," Marshall grinned stupidly. "Thanks."

Rose giggled girlishly and gestured again. "You get along now. Scoot!"

Marshall jumped a little and hurried toward her buildings. As he passed, Rose slapped him on the rear-end causing him to jump. She smiled watching him go, and once he was out of sight, her expression turned icy and she spoke to Jake. "We get one more whiff of trouble, you're going to Texada."

"Yes, ma'am," Jake said.

Rose's eyes narrowed, cold and calculating.

CHAPTER FIFTEEN

A clean, brand new car sat on the road a mile from the speakeasy facing the hill toward town with his's engine cap open. The car looked out of place in the thin layer of muddy snow and dark trees. It shone brightly in the sunlight. Seated in the passenger's side was a beautiful young woman with long, blonde hair and well-cared for clothes. She primped herself using the car's mirror. After a moment, she rubbed her hands together and blew into them. She craned about glancing up and down the road. She sighed and slumped back in her seat.

Down the road a short distance a figure appeared. It was strolling cockily toward the odd vehicle. It was Samuel Shea. He was in much nicer clothes than he had been the night he had attacked Fergus. He had clearly been spending his hard earned wages. He gave a wave and a whistle, drawing the attention of the chilly maiden in the nice car. "Good afternoon, miaa! Do you need help?"

The woman lit up excitedly. She smiled and waved daintily. As he reached the vehicle, she lowered the window with a sweet almost seductive smile. "Oh, yes, yes," she spoke anxiously. "My husband and I were on our way to the inn when we started having engine troubles a few miles away. I don't know exactly what happened, but the car just died right here. I could really use a big, strong man to stay with me while he's getting help."

Samuel cocked an eyebrow. He surveyed the car; it was an impressive vehicle, certainly bought by someone doing quite well for themselves. He looked at the woman, in particular her hands, where several large jewels sat embedded in golden rings. Sam grinned. He knew an opportunity when he saw one. He adjusted the waist of his pants and tucked his revolver to the side so he could lift his foot and place it on the side runner of the car. He leaned against the vehicle and licked his lips. "Well, miss, I would be happy to oblige, if you'll have me."

The woman drew a nervous breath and giggled. She nodded, visibly relieved. "Oh, thank God. I always knew you Texada folk were nice people." She opened the door and slide over on the front seat creating space for Samuel.

Sam looked up and down the road, giddy from his luck. He obliged and climbed into the car, taking his place next to the enchanting beauty. "I must admit, I've not seen such a nice car before."

"Oh, my husband spends so extravagantly. He says it's," she mocks a deep voice, "The finest car in the world." She giggled at herself. "I believe it's a Duesenberg."

Samuel was barely listening. He was taking in the impressive car and the clear wealth of his mark.

"Gosh, it's so cold. Feels like winter already," the woman said and scooted closer to Samuel. He looked at her with surprise, and she hesitated. "I hope you don't mind. I've been sitting here for an hour now. I'm quite chilled."

Samuel smirked. "I don't know if your husband would approve of you being so close to a stranger."

"Well," she extended her hand to him. "I'm Carol."

Samuel took her hand tentatively, shaking it. "Samuel."

"There, you see? You're not a stranger anymore. You're a kind, handsome young man named Samuel," she said and scooted right up next to him getting comfortable. Sam licked his lips hungrily, though still unsure. "Go on, now," Carol said with a titter. "Don't be shy. We're not strangers anymore, remember?"

Sam hesitated but shrugged with a chuckle. What the hell? Why not, he thought, and put his arm around her. She cuddled in reciprocation.

"Oh, thank you so much. You're my hero. You're helping me forget my whole ordeal."

Sam puffed his chest proudly. "Yeah, well, that's me. I just have that effect on women. What can I say?"

"You must be a local legend. Do you know this area well?" Carol asked.

"I do," Samuel said. "See, this here is my road."

"Oh?"

"Yep. People come this way, they gotta pay the toll."

"Really?" Carol said with awe. "So anyone who travels this way pays you?"

"Whether they want to or not," Samuel chuckled wickedly.

"Oh my," Carol laughed and squeezed his arm. "You rogue."

Samuel shrugged and rocked his head back and forth. "A man's gotta maintain a certain lifestyle."

Carol looked up at him, her eyes wide and seductive. "Amazing," she said, her breath warm on Samuel's neck.

Sam looked down into her gorgeous, twinkling eyes. For the first time, he took a good, long look at her. She was wearing makeup and her hair was styled. What was someone so fancy doing out here on the road in such a nice car? Why was she being so forward? It was odd. Samuel swallowed and shifted away from her a few centimeters.

"Is something wrong?" Carol asked.

Sam looked through the windshield. This was all too good to be true. He pulled his arm out from around her and narrowed his eyes. "Where do you suppose your husband is? I didn't see anyone when I came this way. What's taking him so long?" Carol bit her lip. Samuel's mind caught up to the moment. "Did you say this was a Duesenberg?"

Carol's well practiced smile faltered, and her eyes flicked off Samuel and into the backseat. His eyes widened at the glance. He only had an instant to react. He spun around in his seat and froze as Fergus Bradshaw sprang up from hiding and punched Samuel across the face with a pistol held tightly in his meaty hand.

The woman screamed in fright. Samuel's head bounced off the dashboard, and as it ricocheted back, Bradshaw grabbed Sam by his hair and yanked his head down over the back of the seat and threw an arm around his throat. Samuel's neck strained from the force, and his arms and legs flailed. Bradshaw shoved the tip of the pistol into the side of Sam's head.

"Oh, God," Samuel choked. "God, not you!"

Carol scrambled as far from the two men as she was able in the front seat.

Bradshaw's mouth was right beside Samuel's head, and his hot breath and spittle flicked against the struggling man's face as he growled like an animal, "Spending my money? Throwing it around like you're some goddamn gangster?"

Samuel writhed in pain. Bradshaw forced the door open and dragged Sam over the seat and from the car, his limbs scraping and clawing at anything he could touch. Bradshaw was too strong. He threw Samuel to the ground and kicked him in the chest. He began stomping on Samuel's body, catching his arms and stomach, and groin. Samuel grunted and spit with each blow.

Bradshaw ceased his attack and began pacing like an animal. Samuel moaned on the muddy ground, his fine clothes now torn and stained. He tried to crawl away, but he was in too much pain. He coughed up blood as he spoke in hoarse gasps, "Look, I'll-I'll go g-get your m-m-money. I'll g-get it for you right now! I-I haven't spent all of it. Just-just let me go." He flopped over on his back.

Bradshaw's eyes were wide and furious. "You, your posse, and your boss Calloway better watch yourselves. There's a new king on Texada Island!"

Samuel twitched. "C-Calloway? The hell you t-t-talking?" I'm not with no Calloway."

Bradshaw lashed out and kicked Samuel across the head. "Shut up!" Samuel flopped over. He coughed violently into the mud; blood streamed from his mouth. Bradshaw knelt and pushed the tip of the gun into Samuel's temple. "I ain't sorry about this, but someone has to be an example."

Samuel's voice was wet and gurgling, "No, please—"

BLAM! Bradshaw pulled the trigger exploding Samuel's brain and skull into the mud.

Birds took flight from the trees nearby, and the echo of the single shot drifted away on the wind with the flapping wings. Bradshaw frisked the corpse and pulled out a billfold. He stood and slipped his revolver into his belt. His breath was coming in gulps as though he'd just run a mile. He peeled several notes from the billfold and leaned into the car.

Carol was pinned to the far side of the driver's side with her hands over her mouth. She didn't look terrified, but rather simply shocked by the violence. In her line of work, she'd seen plenty of men die.

Bradshaw held out the notes between two fingers and wagged them at her. "Good work, honey," he said.

She took the money and tucked it into her small purse. She looked at the man before her. "That wasn't pretty," she said. Her voice was no longer sweet. It had a twang and an accent that spoke of her life on the streets working corners and making money with her body. "You sure you don't want to come back to the inn with me? I'd be happy to cut a deal."

"We're done here," Bradshaw grunted. He walked around the front of his car and slammed the hood shut. He walked to the driver's side, and Carol slid over as he climbed in and started the engine. He paused and pulled out several more notes. He held them out to the prostitute.

"What's this for? Changing your mind?"

"Your silence," Bradshaw said with a growl. "You breathe a word to anyone, and you won't be breathing at all."

She accepted the money without hesitation. "My lips are sealed."

Bradshaw didn't offer her a second glance. He shoved the car in gear and rumbled toward town. In the muddy road, the lifeless heap that had been Samuel Shea lay crumpled.

CHAPTER SIXTEEN

In the early years of the 19th century, the country of Romania discovered an ally in Canada after the Minister of Home Affairs, Clifford Sifton, representing a Liberal government, had visited Bukovina and promised to populate the West. At the beginning of the century, a group of wealthy and industrious Romanians established themselves throughout the Great White North, from Assiniboia (now Saskatchewan) to British Columbia, at Sifton's advice. Of the first two affluent Romanian families that migrated to Canada from the Bukovina village of Boian, one stopped in Alberta, while the second made their home in the west, more specifically, on the largest island in the Strait of Georgia, Texada Island. The Dalca family formed what would become the thriving logging industry in western Canada.

The Dalcas, under the keen mind of the patriarch of the family, Marius, became the very heart of Texada, establishing trade routes with America and portions of Asia and Europe. They were also responsible for the discovery of large deposits of iron ore, which were eventually used in the construction of Seattle built battleships, the USS Oregon, for the Great White Fleet. The family was treasured for their generosity, though many thought of the daughter of the family to be quite icy in comparison to her parents.

Elizabeth Esme Dulca was the second generation matriarch of the Dalcas after her father's passing, and under her brilliant acumen, she helped establish a firm relationship with the National Canadian Government that would lead to the wartime effort of logging for the military. Bessie had a sharp intellect and an even sharper wit; she was cold, calculating, and not a woman to be reckoned with, which was what made her daughter Theodora such a surprising young woman to those on the island who knew the family.

At seventeen, Theodora fell in love with a low-class logger and abandoned her family's wealth to live in what Bess considered squalor, yet what Theodora assured her was a life full of love and happiness. The two argued frequently, and as it was rumored by the house staff of Bessie's estate, Theodora had inherited her mother's keen mind and would regularly win the arguments. Bess attempted time and again to bring her daughter back into the family business, to abandon her foolish infatuation, or to simply move home again, but Theodora refused the money her family could provide. She wanted to live on her own merits with the man she loved, and though Bess refused to believe her daughter was ever truly happy, when her grandson was born, she was determined to keep her family together. She had all but lost her daughter to a commoner's life, but there was hope that her grandson could grow to be a respectable and higher class of man than his irresponsible father.

When Theodora passed away, Bessie had provided every opportunity she could make available to her grandson. She had seen to it that he was raised with proper schooling and every health benefit. As he grew into a smart, responsible young man, she made certain that he was accepted into the University of British Columbia, a rising prestigious university at the time. She had raised him with class and sophistication. He was the sort of child Bess had hoped her daughter would become. He was destined for greatness, so it was quite infuriating when his father's foolhardiness seeped out of the boy. He joined the Canadian Army before finishing his second year of university when the Great War broke out in Europe. There was no preventing that recklessness from embedding itself in his genes, and he left the island to return to the Old World her family had left behind decades earlier.

Now, Bessie walked through her opulent home, her hair grey and her face lined with years of life, to the front door to greet her handsome grandson with open arms. She found him standing in the foyer in his military jacket and his spectacles ever-so-slightly askew on his face. She took his cheeks in her warm hands and looked at him with great joy. She looked deeply into his eyes and saw his mother, and she choked back a sob of emotion. "Harrison, my beautiful boy. Come in, come in." She pulled him down to her.

Harry blushed as she smothered him with kisses. "Hello, Grandma."

She embraced him. She pulled back and looked at him once more. "You look pale," she said with a frown, her typical expression.

Harry smiled lovingly. "It's winter, Grandma, what do you expect?"

She lovingly patted his hand and they moved into the house–toward the sitting room. Bess gave an order to one of her house servants to bring them tea and biscuits, and she had Harry sit close to the large, crackling fireplace to get some warmth in his body. The servant returned and poured tea for both of them as Bessie explained that she had recently rebuilt the east wing of the house to accommodate her newest hobby of learning harpsichord. Harry sipped the soothing tea and nodded respectfully to her antidotes about her instructor being Bulgarian but understanding that Bess was determined to learn the complete works of Elena Asachi.

"Oh, but listen to me going on," Bessie said and set her tea down. "Where have you been? I expected to see you sooner. How long have you been on the Island?"

"About three weeks," Harry said with the proper amount of chagrin. "I wanted to get settled in before I came to visit."

"Well, you know how I worry."

"I know, but I am well. I've been working at the lumber mill. Just a seasonal position, but if I decide to stay, it could become more permanent."

"Oh, I heard about that awfulness with the man they found. Dreadful. Is no one safe anymore?"

Harry nodded sadly. "Yes, that was unfortunate. Just a poor soul who lost his way out in the woods.

Bessie frowned sternly. "Now, I don't want you getting caught up in messes like that, you hear? You don't go wandering off into the woods. This island isn't what it was when you were a boy."

Harry smiled. "I'll be okay. I sit at a desk all day."

"Good. That Curtis DeBruin knows you're best asset is your mind. In the service you gave enough of your life - putting yourself in danger. You have every right to be comfortable and secure now. You ask me, you shouldn't even be working. You can just retire here, and everything you need will be taken care of. Have you given any consideration to my offer?"

Harry bowed his head politely. "I genuinely appreciate it, Grandma, but I need to be active. I can't just relax my days away."

"Hm," Bessie made a noise of disagreement but said, "Well, as long as you are maintaining a respectful lot in life–the sort of reputable work a veteran should have."

Harry stuck out his bottom lip and shrugged with one shoulder. "It's just logging, but I feel like I'm contributing."

"Logging is what built this island and made this family. You go ahead and take pride in that," Bessie said and added as she picked up her tea cup and went to sip from it, "Anything is better than what that no-good father of yours does."

Harry sighed. He was expecting this. "Grandma," he said in a level tone. "let's not talk about Dad."

Bess sipped her tea and set it back on the tea tray in her lap with a clink. "How is your father?"

Harry exhaled through his nose. She was a stubborn woman. "He's…" he wanted to say well, but knew that wasn't entirely the truth. He searched for a proper word for a moment and decided upon, "well."

Bessie crossed her legs and leaned back in her armchair. She steepled her fingers below her chin. "Is he still wasting his life away out in the woods with that 'machine' of his?"

Harry sighed, "Yes."

"Why your mother ever saw fit to run off and marry that man, I will never know."

Harry lowered his head. He sipped his tea. He swallowed and looked at the old woman. "She was always happy, Grandma."

Bessie stubbornly scoffed and took a drink of her tea, always disappointed to hear her daughter wasn't miserable. "Yes, well…"

The fire crackled. The room was warm and cozy. Harry finished his tea and set the cup aside. He picked up a biscuit and nibbled on it.

"What are your Christmas plans?" Bessie asked.

"Dinner with Dad."

Bess clicked her tongue. "The two of you tucked away in that little shack of his? Nonsense. You two should come here. It would be lovely."

Harry tried not to make a face at that. "He probably won't be able to get all the way across the island to come here," Harry said hesitantly.

"Oh?" Bessie looked at her grandson. "And why is that?"

Harry offered carefully, "He had a little... accident recently."

"What sort of accident?"

"Just a little fall. He's bruised pretty good. Doctor said he should just take it easy through the Holidays," Harry replied and reached for another biscuit.

Bessie scrutinized him. He didn't meet her gaze. She read him so easily. "Hmm, well, I can only assume whatever 'accident' he had was his own fault."

Harry shoved the entire biscuit into his mouth so as not to divulge any more details.

Bess continued, "As long as he wasn't mixing it up with the sort of people who are committing all the crimes up and down the island. I'm telling you, Texada has changed. There's some real American mobster activity going on around here."

"Oh, I don't know about that, Grandma," Harry said through his mouthful.

"No, there is. Poor Samuel Shea was murdered not ten miles from here today."

Harry nearly choked on his biscuit. "What? What did you say?"

"Just down the road. The poor man was robbed and shot. I heard all about it from Alexander Zimmerman just before you came over. Terrible thing. The Mounties found him in the middle of the road. They dragged in and released that no-good Marshall Banks about the whole thing; so, I can only assume this has something to do with those awful moonshine makers on the island."

Harry swallowed tensely.

"Do you see what I mean?" Bessie went on. "This island is no better than those America mobster cities now."

Harry was stunned. His face showed it.

"Oh, now I've gone and frightened you," Bess sighed with great exaggeration. "You look pale again. Here, let me get Alice to make you something to eat. It'll make you feel better."

Bessie rose from her armchair. She moved to Harry and kissed him on the head before walking toward the kitchen. "Alice, can you set the dining room table, please?" Bessie said from down the hall.

Harry was left sitting alone, worry etched on his face.

The front door of Abe's shack opened and Harry entered breathlessly. Chip barked at the suddenness of the arrival. Harry looked around as though expecting to find someone or something hidden in the shadows primed for an attack. Instead, he found only his father seated at the kitchen table, lazily cleaning the last of his catch of the day and the radio softly playing "Sweet Georgia Brown."

"Evening, son," Abe offered barely looking up.

"Dad," Harry said winded and worried. "How's it going?"

Abe shrugged. "Oh, you know, passing the time." He finally looked up at his son, noticing the line of sweat on his upper lip and brow. "You okay? Bike ride take it out of ya tonight?"

Harry scanned the shack again and walked to the table. He had a distressed look on his face.

Abe glanced around the cabin, too. "What's wrong?"

Harry looked at his father. "You haven't heard yet, have you?"

"Heard what?" Abe frowned and set his knife aside.

"Sam Shea was killed this afternoon."

Abe leaned back in his chair and looked up at Harry, gobsmacked. "What? What the hell happened?"

Harry nodded. He was still catching his breath. "Mounties aren't exactly sure yet, from what I've heard. All they know is he was shot in the head and his body was just laying in the middle of the road near town."

Abe exhaled, shocked by the news. "They have any suspects?"

Harry paced. "I'm not sure. I heard they brought Marshall Banks in for questioning, though."

Abe's eyes went wide. "Marshall? Well, that's just crazy. Why would they think for one moment that Marshall had anything to do with a murder?"

"He runs moonshine with you, doesn't he?"

"But why would that make him any sort of suspect?"

"I don't know. They already let him go though. Not sure how he got away without them getting a whiff of that moonshine he's always hauling."

Abe relaxed a little with relief. "Well, Marshall always was clever about that. He always has a tin full of mints to swallow if the Mounties ever cross his path. That, or he bribed them," he added with a grin.

Harry frowned, not amused.

"Poor Samuel. His thieving ways finally caught up with him, I reckon," Abe said.

"Thief?" Harry turned to his father on the word. "You think maybe he's the one who robbed Bradshaw?"

Abe stuck out his bottom lip and rubbed his chin mulling that notion over. "Hm. Wouldn't be surprised, tell you the truth."

Harry stopped pacing and wiped his forehead with the back of his hand. The song changed on the radio. Charlie Poole's upbeat "Don't Let Your Deal Go Down Blues" began. Harry took a seat and exhaled, his heart finally slowing down, though his anxiety still high. Abe tapped his foot and wrapped his mind around the news. An anger started to fill him.

"I came here to get away from all this shit," Harry said with disappointment.

"It's that goddamn Bradshaw boy," Abe growled. "He's brought this American gangster mentality to Texada, and I ain't gonna stand for it." He rose, determination on his face.

Harry looked up, surprised by his father's anger.

"Gonna be difficult with the Mounties keeping an eye on my delivery man," Abe said and began to pace the same path Harry had been treading.

"I thought you were enjoying your retirement," Harry said.

Abe snorted. "I said I was *resting*, and for just this little while, It was my Christmas present for you."

"But—"

I ain't got a choice but to get back into it. Only way to see Bradshaw run outta town is to out produce him. Corner the market on the island for Rose."

Harry looked at Abe for a long while.

"Don't look at me like that," Abe said.

"You're impossible, you know that?" Harry scowled. "Bradshaw's murdering people, and you want to piss him off by being a better bootlegger than him?"

Abe pointed at Harry. "Look, life and memories are what you make of them; and, I want to live what's left of mine doing what I love. I'm too old not to do that. I'm sorry for what happened to your friends, but the hard truth is I'm not responsible. The booze isn't responsible; it just happened. It was an accident. All you can do is mourn your losses, dust yourself off, and get on with your life."

Harry lowered his head and was quiet for several breaths. His expression softened and he nodded. "I know," he said quietly. He stood and limped past Abe for the front door.

"Where you going?" Abe asked.

"I think I just need to get some sleep."

"It's getting cold out there now with the snow coming. You don't need to be out at that camp when you could be in here where it's warm."

Harry stopped at the door and nodded thankfully to his dad. "I like being under the stars. It clears my head. Goodnight." With that, he walked out of the shack.

Abe frowned and looked at Chip who was staring at him. "Oh, don't you give me that look, too," Abe grumbled.

Harry walked from the cabin scowling. He started down the path toward his camp and stopped. He looked back at the house, and then down the road. His face was hard, his jaw set. The wind blew, cold and gently. The light dusting of snow shifted around his legs.

A moment later, he was on his bike riding away from the shack.

CHAPTER SEVENTEEN

As the weather turned colder and the fall of snow more frequent, the speakeasy on Texada Island grew more crowded. The loggers and fishers came for the warm fire, lively company, and, of course, the flowing alcohol. Tonight, music blared from the corner band, upbeat and swinging. Couples whipped about doing the Charleston and a new dance that had made its way from the East Coast, Lindy Hop. Hoots and hollers accompanied impressive moves, but more cheers came from the bar where Fergus Bradshaw had just bought a round for everyone in the bar. He revelled in the attention from his hangers-on as he threw his money around. There were several men, a few girls in the mix as well, including Carol, who was pawing all over Earl. It is a drunken, raucous, good time.

The entrance opened, and Harry walked into the joint. No one even bothered to look up or notice him as he stood there and looked around. He took his glasses off and wiped them of the fog that came from coming in from the cold to the warmth. As he slid them back on, his gaze fell upon Bradshaw. Harry shook his jacket of a few flakes of snow and walked to the far end of the bar. The bartender gave him a polite nod. Harry ordered a sarsaparilla. The bartender set the bottle in front of him and returned to the party at the other end of the bar.

"To the continued success of Texada's newest son and entrepreneur!" Earl declared and raised his glass. The crowd cheered, and Bradshaw grinned and waved. All, that is except for Harry.

RJ looked over the head of the woman he was pawing and noticed Harry. "Hey, Earl," RJ grunted and pointed with his chin. "Look at this fella. No love to give Mr. Bradshaw, eh?"

Harry raised his bottle and tilted his head in acknowledgment of the remark.

"You got a problem, fella," RJ snarled.

"Maybe I don't feel the same way all you feel about Texada's newest son," Harry said plainly.

RJ shoved his date aside. "And what's that supposed'ta mean?"

Harry took a long drink, never taking his eyes off RJ. He set the bottle down. "Maybe I don't want to celebrate gangster trash."

Earl sat up and pushed Carol off his lap. "What'd you say, boy?"

The music died down, tension rising in the room. Bradshaw turned, finally noticing his two friends and the newcomer.

"I'm sorry, do you need me to speak slower?" Harry asked sarcastically.

The big man raised a fist. Earl pushed his stool aside scraping the floor. The room drew a collective breath, but before RJ could throw a punch, Bradshaw stepped to his side and grabbed his wrist stopping the blow. RJ glared at Harry, but Harry didn't even flinch.

Bradshaw clapped Earl and RJ on the shoulders and said jovially, "Boys, I think that's enough celebration for the night. Don't you have somewhere to be?"

Earl shot his boss a look of disappointment. "Aw, come on, Fergus. We was just getting comfortable."

"And now you're getting gone," Bradshaw said with a menacing smile. "Move, before I lose my temper."

Earl frowned, shot a look at Harry, and then slapped the back of his hand on RJ's chest. "Alright, alright. Come on." He smiled at Carol one last time and leaned to give her a kiss. She turned her head and put her hand on his face.

The room laughed.

"Time's up, Sugar. Come back when you have some more scratch to throw around," Carol said sweetly.

The men laughed even harder. Earl glowered, turned, and stomped from the bar, sending one more contemptuous glare at Harry. "Be seeing ya, kid," he said before breezing out the door with RJ in tow.

Bradshaw called to the bartender, "Another round! And make it from my supply! This party needs a kick in the ass!"

The sycophantic group cheered, and the music kicked back into full gear. Bradshaw beamed, so proud of his collection of supporters. He puffed his chest and soaked it in before siddling over to Harry and pulling up a stool beside him. "I like your style, fella. Not everyone has the stones to talk like that to RJ," Bradshaw said. "You a logger, eh?"

"Yes," Harry replied and didn't even bother to look at the other man.

Bradshaw grinned even wider. He shook his head in amusement and sipped his drink. He winced and licked his lips. He turned on the stool to face this strange fellow more fully. "You ain't the type to be intimidated, are you?"

Harry nodded once. "No."

Bradshaw narrowed his eyes, scanning Harry. "You fight in the War?"

Harry offered a single nod again, though he didn't reply audibly this time.

Bradshaw sipped his drink. He pointed. "You on the island or just passing through?"

"On the island."

Bradshaw kept smiling, impressed by the blunt stranger. "You know, I'm always looking for men like you for my company."

Harry finally glanced at Bradshaw with a raised eyebrow. "Oh?"

Bradshaw puffed his chest impressively. "It's a budding and flourishing business. Unfortunately, it draws the attention of some... undesirable people, from time to time."

"Like your friends?" Harry said flatly.

Bradshaw barked with laughter. "Haha! Oh, no-no-no. Earl and RJ there are the kinda men who keep the undesirables away. People who try to disrupt what I do. People who try to get in my way. They take care of it."

Harry turned to face the other man. "And how do they do that?" he asked.

Bradshaw leaned in close. His breath was warm and smelled strongly of moonshine. "In whatever way I deem prudent," he sneered and winked.

"Hm," Harry shifted ever-so-slightly in his seat so he couldn't feel Bradshaw's breath on his neck any longer. "So, you're like a general."

Bradshaw liked the sound of that. "Exactly! Like a general. Haha!" He slapped Harry between the shoulderblades.

Harry was not amused. He steadied himself and took a drink from his bottle staring forward again.

Bradshaw scrutinized him and licked his lips. He leaned too closely again. "Which branch you serve in? You were in the Army, weren't ya?" He surveyed Harry up and down. "Yeah, yeah I can see it in your eyes. You gotta bit of the devil in ya, don'tcha?"

Harry replied flatly, "Yes, Army."

Bradshaw narrowed his eyes and his grin became wicked. "I'd love to have a man with skill working at my side."

Harry turned and faced the cruel man again, this time with a cold glare. "I served to stop cruel and dangerous men like you, Fergus," he hissed.

Bradshaw's smile dropped. He stared at the stranger before him, a palpable tension between the two men. "What's your name, soldier?"

"Calloway. Harry Calloway."

Bradshaw laughed loudly and cruelly. "Abe's got a boy, eh? Heh-heh-heh. And his boy's got an ax to grind, don't he?"

Harry flexed his fists. His heart raced.

Bradshaw sneered, still smiling. "Ain't nothing but business between me and your pop."

"Like it was with Sam Shea?"

Bradshaw's eyes flicked to the bar, a momentary concern that quickly went away. "You know," he said menacingly. "it is a bit like that, ain't it?"

Harry stared daggers at the man. Bradshaw bared his teeth in a wide, wicked smile. After a moment, the bigger man rose from his stool and pulled out a wad of cash. He slapped a couple notes on the bar with his meaty hand. "Hey, Arlo," he said pointing at Harry with his chin. "This one's on me."

He leaned back toward Harry. Their eyes locked on one another. "Enjoy your night," Bradshaw smirked with malice. "I suspect we'll be seeing each other again real soon."

Harry's lip twitched, but he didn't say a word.

The gangster turned to the speakeasy. "Come on, y'all! Let's take this celebration to the farm. Got a fresh batch of refreshments I'd love for you all to try."

Once more, the crowd celebrated Bradshaw, and they all quickly filed out the front door into the night for further debauchery.

Harry sat alone at the bar, only Arlo, the bartender remained wiping down a tabletop and collecting mugs. After a moment, he didn't know how long, Harry exhaled and finally opened his clenched fist. He had squeezed so hard that he'd drawn blood from his palm. He looked down at the tiny droplets and sighed. He relaxed, though the anger in him was still clear.

CHAPTER EIGHTEEN

The stars were slowly consumed by the thick clouds crawling through the blanket of inky black. The wind picked up. A storm was coming, and Marshall Banks shivered as he rowed his boat up to the shore where Abe and Chip stood waiting on the dock, the old man wearing a thick jacket zipped all the way to his chin. Abe signaled him with a low whistle, and Marshall waved his lantern to signal his approach. The boat knocked against the wood planks, and Abe reached out a friendly hand to help Marshall onto the dock. On the shore, Abe's truck sat in wait, a single barrel and five crates of mason jars rested in the truck bed.

"Heard you had a conversation with the Mounties," Abe said. His breath came out in puffs of white.

"Yep," Marshall grunted more annoyed than upset. "You heard about Sam Shea, then, eh?"

"I did," Abe said, and they walked to the truck and began unloading the barrel and crates of moonshine.

"It was just down the road from my place. I was the closest neighbor, so they were wondering if I'd seen anything."

"And did you?" Abe asked.

"No," Marshall grunted as he lifted one of the heavier crates off the truck bed. "But I'd put dimes to doggies it was Bradshaw."

"Me too," Abe said darkly. "We gotta be careful."

"Don't I know it," Marshall said grimly.

They look out over the dark waters. Abe squinted at the shadows. "Anyone see you rowing in?"

"No, I took the east shoreline. Lots of overhanging trees to hide among," Marshall said.

Abe stuck his bottom lip out and nodded satisfied.

Marshall set down his crate on the dock near the boat and wiped his brow. Despite the cold, he was sweating from the exertion or maybe his nerves. He lifted his lantern from the boat and finally took a good look at his friend. He smiled. "Good to see you up and at 'em again, by the by. You're healing nicely. You're no prettier than you ever were, though."

Abe made a face–a frown at the jest. He smirked and shook his head. He looked out at the dark swamp again and considered the quiet. "You're sure no one saw you?"
"I'm sure," Marshall said and then immediately started doubting himself, his nervous nature overcoming his levity. He looked out into the night from whence he came. "I mean, I'm pretty sure." He looked at Abe. "A little jumpy now, eh?"

Abe didn't reply. He stared, the bruises on his cheek highlighted in the lantern light. The two men stood in silence, Marshall rang his hands, and Abe scrutinized every shadow. Chip sniffed the wind.

Abe accepted the quiet and exhaled. They bent down and loaded the booze into Marshall's boat. As they dropped the last crate, Abe gripped his friend's shoulder. "Alright. Be careful out there. You never know who's going to be watching. You sure you want to take these to the Malahat solo tonight?" He gestured to the barrel and crates.

Marshall nodded. "Yeah. Easier to miss one man than two. Go rest up, Abe. I'll see you in a little while."

"Come by as soon as you're back," Abe said. He stepped back as Marshall dropped into his boat. Chip gave a single yip, and a moment later, Marshall was drifting back into the cold waters.

The swamp river twisted and turned west, and soon, Marshall was gliding out into open water. He remained along the shore moving south, keeping close to the overhanging trees. He hummed to himself as he passed several night fisherman using candles to draw in the fish. He waved politely. With the supply tucked under a tarp, to them, Marshall was just another fisherman. After half a mile, he turned away from the shore and made his way to deeper waters in the Strait of Georgia..

It was a calm night on the Strait, though the winter chill still bit at Marshall's skin. He pulled his coat tighter around his neck and paused. His ears had caught something in the wind. Faint voices. Marshall squinted at the dark. Someone was talking nearby. He couldn't make out much, but he did pick two words from the sound: "He's coming." Marshall's eyes widened. And then a gunshot rang out!

On instinct, Marshall threw himself to his stomach on the bottom of his boat. "Shit!" he yelped. He made himself as flat as possible. "Oh, Lord, save my ass," he whimpered. BLAM-BLAM!! Another two shots, and this time, bullets bit into the wood of the boat. Another bullet sounded and tinged off the keg. Marshall flinched at every shot. He made a desperate choice, grabbed the oars, and began to row in a desperate panic. He used the keg as cover. He was shaking in terror, but he rowed with all his might. More shots came, but they sounded more faint. He was putting distance between himself and his attackers.

"Banks!" came a furious voice. "Consider yourself warned, you son of a bitch! You haul for anyone but Bradshaw again, and we'll kill you!" The voice echoed.

Marshall shook uncontrollably, but he kept rowing. His breath came in gulps. His arms stung. He was exhausted, but he didn't stop pushing himself until the Malahat was in clear view, and even then, once on board, he didn't stop shaking for an hour.

The sun was already coloring the eastern horizon as Marshall rolled the keg beside the stack of mason jar crates. He let it thunk to the wood, and he sat down. He was exhausted. His eyes had purple circles under them, and he just wanted to sleep. He rubbed his face as Boss Rose surveyed the hall; Jake stood like a statue up the pier a bit, arms crossed over his chest eyeing Marshall.

Rose took a sip of one of Abe's jars and smacked her lips in satisfaction. "Abe continues to amaze me."

"Yeah," Marshall said tiredly. "He's one of the good ones, ma'am."

"It's even better than his last." Rose strolled closer to him. She took the tip of her well-shone boots and tapped the keg under Marshall. "Care to tell me what happened here?"

Marshall looked down at the two bullet holes in the keg. Amber liquid drizzled down the metal barrel. He bit his lip nervously and tried to meet Rose's gaze. "Oh, um…"

"This why you were late?" she spoke in a light tone, almost carefree.

Marshall squirmed and rang his hands. "Er, yeah, about that. Just a little trouble with some locals, Boss."

Rose was not amused. She put a hand on Marshall's shoulder and moved it to his neck. It was a gentle touch, but Marshall tensed. "Locals?" she asked in the same light tone.

Marshall swallowed. "Y-yes, Boss. I didn't see 'em, but-but-but they were shooting at me."

"Oh my," Rose said with feigned concern. She shifted her hand and softly caressed Marshall's Adam's apple with her thumb. "Who were these men?"

"Just some men," Marshall stammered. "Th-they said they was working for Fergus Bradshaw."

Rose's face grew dark. Her thumb pushed slightly on Marshall's throat.

Marshall yelped, "He don't want me running for Abe no more."

Rose smiled humorlessly. She released the poor man's neck and gently tapped the side of his face with her gloved hand. She turned and took a casual step toward Jake. "That damn man. Is he just that thick-headed?"

Jake 's jaw tightened.

"It might not've been Bradshaw," Marshall said quickly but then added lamely, "Even if they specifically said his name and all." He stood from the barrel. "I just–I don't think it would be the local toughs. They're shaken up since one of their own was killed last week. And people think Bradshaw did it."

Boss Rose clicked her tongue in disapproval. "And Texada used to be such a wholesome piece of heaven."

Marshall laughed nervously. "Heh, yeah." He cleared his throat. "Frankly, ma'am, it got bad when Bradshaw took over from his father. He's not from Canada, anyway. Really giving Americans a bad name, if you ask me." Adding quickly, "No offense."

Rose drew a long breath of the chilly morning air and blew it slowly through her lips. "Agreed. Not acceptable. Not acceptable at all," she said in dismay. "I'm disappointed in that young man." She turned and faced Marshall. "You didn't short them, did you?"

Marshall eyes widened. His tone rose in defense. "What? No, ma'am, I gave them the pay you've approved, every time, without fail. They just don't want the competition with Abe. Shooting at me like I'm some sort of two-timing smuggler or thief–"

Rose's look at the word was like a slap. Her eyes widened. "Thief?"

Marshall twitched, flustered.

Rose's head tilted haughty. "Marshall Banks, you're not playing games with my white lightning, are you?"

Marshall babbled quickly, "N-no, ma'am! I wouldn't dream of it. I don't know why I said that. I'm just saying, they was shooting at me like-like-like I'm some rat."

Rose raised her eyebrows. Jake's hand moved to his hip and the lump of a pistol there.

Marshall kept rambling, "And I'm not! I wouldn't short no one. I wouldn't undermining anyone." He licked his lips and rang his hands skittishly. "Especially someone who had Jake Edwards working beside them. That's why I'm telling you this. I'm not smuggling nothing other than what I run for you. I ain't short Bradshaw or no one. I do my job, just like you ask me to. Every time. No muss or fuss. Honest."

Rose smiled snakelike. "Good. Because if you do short someone like Bradshaw, you short *me* of my product. And you don't want to know what happens when I get wind of that kind of trickery."

Jake's hand rested on the lump under his coat. Marshall was visibly trembling.

"I know! I-I wouldn't dream of crossing you. Honest! Okay?"

Rose knew the power she had over the poor man–the power she had over her entire operation. She continued to smile placidly. "Very good." She set her hand on the crate of mason jars and rolled her fingers. "Very well. Off you go," she said to Marshall. "Stick to the north coast landing. The going is harder, but it's more remote. Whether it was Bradshaw's men or not, I can't afford to have anyone taking potshots at you."

Marshall shifted uncertainty. Boss Rose shooed him away with a flick of her hand, and he clambered up the gangplank back to the Malahat. Rose rocked her head back and forth in thought watching the jittery smuggler vanish onto the boat. She looked up at the sky, the light blue of the morning light illuminating the dock.

Jake came to her side. "What do you want me to do?"

Rose watched the Malahat drift off to the open Ocean. "Go," she said. "See how this plays out. If Jimmy's boy can't keep his shit together, explain to him how this business works."

"Yes, ma'am," Jake said and moved to depart.

"And Jake," she turned to face him. "Use your own discretion."

Jake lowered his head respectfully and headed off toward the warehouse. Rose looked out once more at the ship, now small in the distance. Her eyes narrowed askance.

Chip barked as Abe walked out onto the porch carrying his fishing pole. The late afternoon sun had melted away most of the frost covering the trees and grass. He looked up to see Marshall coming down the path to the house; Abe made a thoughtful noise and waved to his friend. "Afternoon. Wasn't expecting you until Saturday. Quick trip."

"Hey-ya, Abe. Yeah, in a manner of speaking," Marshall said. His color was still drained from his face.

"Rough waters last night? You look a little green around the gills," Abe remarked.

"I got shot at last night," Marshall said with a tremble in his voice. "Bradshaw's men."

Abe's eyes widened. "Jesus, Marsh. Are you okay?"

"Rattled," Marshall said. "They were out on the Strait in boats, waiting for me."

"Christ," Abe blew threw his lips in shock. "The batch?"

"Saved it. Rose was mighty peeved I was late with it, but it's better than having lost it all at sea."

Abe clenched his jaw. "Those sons of bitches."

"I think they were just trying to scare me," Marshall said with a weak smile. "It worked."

Abe squeezed his fishing rod. "Goddammit. I should've been with you. I knew something felt off.."

"There was nothing you could've done 'cept hunker down in that rickety old boat beside me."

"Did they say anything?"

"They don't want me to take your whiskey anymore is what it is. Bradshaw's claiming the territory."

Abe sighed and shook his head. His mind was turning it all over.

Marshall went on, "Not sure how they expect me to run for anyone. I got holes in my boat. It's not seaworthy anymore; I'm surprised I got to the Malahat without sinking." He rubbed the back of his neck. "And Rose looked like she was gonna let Jake Edwards gut me right then and there. We are in a bad, bad spot here, Abe. How am I gonna keep going when they got my route covered?"

Abe was frustrated, and his face showed it. He rubbed his jaw in thought. "Not necessarily. I have connections with some of the trawler captains. Citron and Matthews, Burzelic." He narrowed his eyes in thought. "We got options."

"Would they ferry out the booze?"

"They might."

"And you trust 'em?"

Abe considered that a moment.

"Abe," Marshall said warningly. "They gotta be straight. You don't want to risk it all on some rat."

"You leave that to me. Next delivery, instead of meeting me on the beach, bring your truck here."

Marshall was hesitant. "I dunno, partner. I mean, I got guys shooting at me? They're killing people like Sam. Are you sure you wanna do this?"

Abe said determinedly, "Yes." He looked at his worried friend. "But if you're not up to it, I won't blame you."

Marshall looked at the ground and shuffled his feet. He took a breath and let it go in long exhale. "If you think we can make this work, I want to help."

Abe put a hand on Marshall's shoulder. "I'll take care of everything. I promise." He turned back to the shack. "Now, come on.I got the still brewing. I'm gonna put some extra love into this batch."

Marshall kicked at the ground, reluctantly convinced by his old friend, and followed him into the house, patting Chip on the head as he passed the dog.

Chip sat on the porch watching the men enter the house. He wagged his tail and looked out at the trees, tongue hanging from his mouth happily.

CHAPTER NINETEEN

The sun was dipping low as the end of the day approached. Harry was frying fish for dinner on his campfire when Abe rapped his knuckles on a tree at the end of the path announcing himself, "Hey there."

Hello," Harry replied with a smile. "Just getting supper going. Care for some salmon? Got plenty. Chip can even have some, if he's up for it."

"I'm sure he's thrilled," Abe chuckled. "Where is he?"

Harry cocked his head. "He's not with you?"

Abe frowned. "What do you mean? I thought he was over here with you." He peered around the camp.

Harry stood, worry growing on his face. "He's not lost, is he?"

"I don't think so. He knows his way around here better than either of us," Abe said and furrowed his brow. "I left him on the porch a few hours ago. I just saw Marshall off and figured he came down here to visit."

Harry took his skillet off the fire and set his fish aside. He pulled his jacket on and reached behind the log he was seated upon, bringing up a rifle.

"What are you doing?" Abe asked.

"We've got to go find Chip," Harry said with all seriousness.

Abe scoffed. "Come on now. He'll show up." He whistled and cupped his hands over his mouth. "Hey, Chip! Come on out, boy!"

Harry shook his head. "With all that's happening around here, You wanna just wait around?"

Abe considered that for a moment, his thoughts turning to Marshall's incident on the Strait. Abe's heart began to pound. He was suddenly quite worried. "Let's go."

They trekked away from Harry's camp and into the forest. The sun was getting lower in the sky. It would be night in the next hour. Harry kept his rifle raised, his eyes sharp. Abe whistled every now and again calling out the old pup's name. Birds who had yet to travel south took flight from the loud calls and their tromping feet, but there was no sign of Chip.

They entered a clearing. Harry turned a wide circle not sure which way to continue searching. "It's getting dark," he said.

"Where is that dog?" Abe asked the wind.

"He wouldn't run off, would he?"

Abe thought a moment. A soft smile crept over his face and he chuckled at some thought.

"What?" Harry asked bemused.

"Maybe that's it," Abe said with another chuckle. "Maybe he ran off. I was just picturing him chasing some damn squirrel, jumping aboard a fishing boat, and taking a holiday away from the island."

"Well, that would certainly be something," Harry laughed.

They both stood grinning at the thought, but suddenly stopped short when the cold wind blew across the clearing. In it, they could hear a pained whine. Abe turned sharply to the sound. "Did you hear that?"

Harry nodded and raised his rifle. "It's coming from over there. Come on!"

They ran through the trees following the sound. Abe shouted, "Chip! Chip, speak, boy! Speak!"

From just ahead, Chip barked weakly. Harry and Abe burst from the trees onto a creekbed, where they found Chip stuck in a large wire snare. The poor dog was quivering, the wire wrapped around his rear, blood and snowy mud making his fur slick.

Abe fell to his knees beside his friend. "Chip! God, are you okay?" he saw the blood. "Whose snare is this?" He began to attempt to loosen the wire as Chip whimpered mournfully.

"I don't know," Harry said and knelt beside them setting his rifle aside. "Let me get it." He pulled out a hunting knife and cut Chip free. Chip looked up to them with big, round eyes and wagged his tail weakly.

"Easy, boy, easy. You're safe now," Abe said. The old man had a tear at the corner of his eye, pained to see his friend so hurt. "Who did this to you?"

Harry clenched his jaw. There was a darkness brewing in him. "Bradshaw," he said through his teeth and rose to standing putting his knife away and taking up his rifle once more.

Abe looked at Harry. "Maybe," Abe said, though he knew it was more likely than anything. "Son of a bitch." He cradled Chip's head. "I suppose it could have been a trapper. Plenty around here. Could've been an accident—"

"It has to be him!" Harry said forcefully and pointed a sharp finger at the snare. "Look how it was set up. No one uses snares like this; it's sloppy."

Abe muttered angrily, ""Dammit…"

"They're trying to hurt you," Harry said seriously.

Abe opened his mouth to reply when a loud snap of a branch came from ahead of them over the creek. They looked up sharply, and Harry's keen eyes spotted a figure bracing a rifle on his shoulder.

Harry shouted, "Sniper!"

"What are you—" Abe began but was cut short as Harry tackled him to the ground just as a loud shot rang out.

The wind was knocked from Abe. Harry expertly rolled onto his stomach into a prone position, brought his rifle up and aimed at the treeline. He used his arm to slide his glasses more securely to his face and looked down the sight of his gun. He recognized the man running away. Harry steadied his breath and placed his finger on the trigger. "It's that bastard, Earl Martin," he said calmly and flexed his index finger—

BLAM! Another shot rang out but not from Harry's gun. The wood of a tree three feet from the Calloways was chopped by the bullet from another gunman behind them. Harry and Abe ducked, Abe throwing himself over Chip.

"Second man!" Harry shouted.

"Gotta be RJ," Abe said.

"It was a wild shot," Harry said with certainty. "He doesn't have a good position on us. Come on!"

Harry yanked his father to his feet and up the slight embankment. Abe cradled Chip in his arms like a child. Harry pushed Abe into a run and kept his rifle sweeping the trees. Harry ran with very little limp, the adrenaline coursing through him. "Go! Get to the trees!"

They ran for it, though Abe struggled, slower than his son. "What do we do now? I can't run like this for long," he said breathlessly.

"There!" Harry pointed. "In that thicket."

They ducked into thick brush and a large fallen tree. Harry braced his back against the log and checked the rifle. Abe pet Chip soothingly, shushing him. It was a momentary reprieve.

"We should circle back to the house," Abe said.

"No," Harry said. "We run 'em east. I got a hunting pit about 200 meters that way." He peered over the tree, his tone and body as calm as ever.

Abe looked at his son and saw the soldier for the first time. It was impressive; Abe could not deny it.

Somewhere in the distance, Earl and RJ converged. RJ pointed in the direction he saw their targets flee. Earl nodded. They reloaded their rifles and slowly advanced, ready for another volley. They took several steps, before—

A blur and snapping branches fifty meters to their left. They whip around and spot Harry sprinting through the brush and tree trunks. Earl fires a wild shot, missing Harry and tearing open a thin tree like a banana roughly being broken in half.

"Come on!" Earl said and hurried forward.

Harry hurled himself forward through the wilderness with familiarity. His hands were empty. He came upon a cluster of pine trees and jumped over a subtly marked hunting pit at their base. As his feet left the ground, kicking flecks of mud with the effort, another shot rang out. He threw his hands over his head as he landed. He ducked and fell, not struck, but rolling. He flopped through the mud and small collection of snow and scrambled for cover behind a stump.

BLAM! Another shot. This one struck the tree stump too near Harry's head.

Harry jerked away from the splintering wood.

Earl and RJ thundered through the trees, both of them keeping their rifles up and ready. They came to the pine trees and took pause. Earl sneered and shouted, "You got spirit, boy! Now, why don't I send that spirit on?"

RJ took one more step, but his foot found no purchase. He rocked forward and violently tumbled into the cleverly disguised storage pit. His face struck the hard-pack dirt on the way down. He landed in a heap in an instant.

Earl reeled around to see his friend laying in the pit when Abe leaped out from behind him and fired a shot from Harry's rifle directly into Earl's leg. Earl screamed and whipped about firing a shot right back at Abe and striking the old man in the waist.

"Ah!" Abe grunted and fell to the ground.

Earl fell as well, directly into the pit beside RJ, who was groaning half conscious and bleeding from his face. Earl maintained his senses and flipped about to a sitting position. He gripped his leg and screamed in agony, "You son of a bitch! You can't escape forever, Calloway!" his words were slurred.

Harry scrambled to his father. Abe was breathing, but he was bleeding heavily. "Shit," Harry said as he slid to his knees beside Abe.

In the pit, Earl gritted his teeth and cursed through his pain. His eyes drooped, and before he could launch another volley of expletives, unconsciousness overtook him.

Abe stirred and tried to sit up, but the agony was too much. He cried out painfully.

"Lay back down," Harry ordered. "I'm going for help."

"I can't feel my legs," Abe grunted.

"Just lay still. I'll be right back. Stay still."

Abe nodded weakly and tilted his head back. Harry got to his feet and took off into the forest as fast as his legs would allow. His limp was quite severe now that his initial burst of adrenaline was fading.

"You got a damn doctor for me?" Earl snarled as the Mounties walked him down the forest path and onto the road where a paddy wagon was waiting. His leg was bleeding, but he was able to walk.

"You seem fine to me." The Mountie shoved Earl between the shoulders and into the rear of the police van.

He and RJ were being escorted away by two lawmen while Doctor Zimmerman, a silver-haired gentleman with deep lines on his brow, examined Abe. Harry stood in the road, the Mounties loading their assailants into the vehicle to his right, Abe and the doctor to his left. Chip was fast asleep in the front seat of the truck, his paw over his eyes in a very human gesture.

Abe was seated in the bed of his truck. Harry had used it to lead the Mounties to the woods. Abe was bandaged around the waist and back. The color was gone from his face, and he winced when he moved.

Doc Zimmerman took a pen and prodded Abe's feet and legs. "How about now?" he asked.

"Nothing," Abe replied grimly. A horrible realization was washing over him. "I can't even move 'em." He bit his lip in pain and growing anger.

Zimmerman put his pen in his front pocket. He spoke levelly, "Stay calm, Abe. We've got the bleeding under control. Don't assume the worst. Your legs not moving could be temporary. We don't know anything for certain just yet."

Abe grunted as he leaned back and onto his side, laying in the truck bed. He stared up at the canopy of trees overhead, sadness and exhaustion all over his face. He shut his eyes, letting sleep take him.

Doc Zimmerman lowered his head sadly and then looked up at Harry in the road. Harry's jaw was clenched tightly. He stared unblinking at his father. The fire in Harry's chest was burning hotter and hotter, like the flame of a still being fanned.

CHAPTER TWENTY

Marshall cupped his hands around his eyes and looked through the front window of Abe's shack. It was dark within. In front of the cabin, Marshall's truck sat with his beaten up old row boat attached to the tail. Marshall leaned back from the window and looked out at the forest with a glum expression.

"Come on, Abe," he muttered. "Where the hell are ya?"

Texada's only hospital was a three-story brick building nestled a mile from the western shore and as old as the island community itself. It had weathered every icy winter and every humid summer since the founding of the city. Anyone who was born on the island had entered the world within the walls of that hospital. It was a landmark that had seen the island grow. It's windows had been the eyes that watched over Texada Island and its people for generations.

Now, the sun beamed through those windows. A hard shaft of light cut through thick curtains and warmed the leg of Harry Calloway seated beside his father's bed reading. In the corner, Harry had brought the radio from the cabin. Jimmie Rodgers warbled "In The Jailhouse Now."

Well I had a friend named Rambling Bob who used to steal gamble and rob
He thought he was the smartest guy in town

But I found out last Monday that Bob got locked up
Sunday
They got him in the jailhouse way downtown…

Abe stirred and opened his eyes, squinting and groaning at the sun. "Hmph," he muttered and put his hand over his eyes. "Too bright."

Harry shut his book and leaned closer to the bed. "Hey, how are you feeling?"

Abe looked around the room and frowned. "Damn," he said. "Thought it might all be a dream."

Harry nodded sadly. He could appreciate the sentiment. He touched his own leg for a moment, recalling his time in the medical tent on the other side of the world.

"Did I at least get that son of a bitch as good as he got me?" Abe asked.

"He won't ever walk straight again. Suppose that's something. Mounties arrested both of them. Locked 'em up."

"Good," Abe said ruefully. "Hopefully they stay that way."

"You don't think they'd get off, do you?" Harry asked worriedly.

Abe adjusted in his bed, propping himself up with his pillow underneath his back. "Money is power. Bradshaw's got plenty of it."

Harry scowled, his cheeks flushing red with frustration and anger. "That's not fair."

Abe put his lips together and raised his brow. That's the way of it, son."

Harry's jaw clenched. The injustice of it filling his chest with heat.

Abe tapped his legs and sighed deeply. He maintained his matter-of-fact tone. "Don't look like I'll ever walk straight again either."

"Doc Zimmerman says there's still a chance it's only temporary," Harry said.

"You believe that?"

Harry shrugged.

Abe closed his eyes and drew a breath through his nose. The breath popped through his lips. "Well, I sure as shit can't live like some cripple," he said harshly. "Son of a bitch should've killed me."

"Hey," Harry said forcefully. "Don't talk that way. You'll be okay. You're lucky to be alive, really."

Abe grimaced and looked away. Harry shared his frustration. They sat in silence for a long moment.

"Merry Christmas," Abe broke the silence sourly.

Harry lowered his head. "Take it a day at a time."

"Yeah, yeah," Abe waved a hand.

More silence.

The door creaked open, and the pair looked up as Jake Edwards walked into the room. Abe's eyes widened. Harry frowned and rose from his seat.

"Excuse me, can we help you?" Harry asked firmly.

Abe grabbed Harry's arm. "Boy, easy now," he warned.

Jake lifted his hands palms out. "I'm just here to talk."

"You know this guy?" Harry asked Abe without taking his eyes off Jake.

"I do," Abe said tensely. "Good to see you, Jake. How's Rose?"

Harry understood immediately. He faced Jake and glared at the man.

Jake stood at the door. "She's fine. Can I have a minute?"

Abe nodded and patted Harry's arm assuring him. "Yeah."

Harry looked at his dad, not sure he wanted to step out of the room; so, he moved to the window and sat on the sill. He was alert, ready if anything were to unfold with this mysterious stranger.

Jake pulled a chair to the other side of Abe's bed and took a seat. Jake was confident, unflappable. There was a power about him, despite his age. Harry couldn't tell how old the man was, but he could see in Jake's icy blue eyes that he had decades of experience, and that experience was clearly criminal and bloody.

"How are you feeling?" Jake asked.

"As good as I look," Abe huffed. "I think my business days might be done though."

Jake folded his thick hands over his barrel chest. "Be a shame to see you retire. Can't really imagine you hanging it up. Fishing and listening to your radio all day. Can't imagine you'd last a week."

Abe scoffed, "You'd be surprised."

Jake smiled. It was a rare, unsettling sight. He sat a moment listening to the Benny Goodman Orchestra play a Christmas medley from the radio. Harry shifted on the window sill.

"This guy Bradshaw," Jake started. "I get the feeling he's none too happy with you. Something about a robbery?"

"He didn't do it," Harry said annoyed.

Jake eyed Harry, examining the young man. "Never thought he did."

"If you work for this Boss Rose, and you know my dad so well, why don't you do something about this?"

Jake held Harry's eyes for a long moment. The old man smacked his lips and said smoothly to Abe, "He's got your spirit, that's for sure." The two old men grinned.

Harry scowled agitated. "Well?"

Jake focused his attention on Abe. "Rose wants this taken care of. She didn't want all this trouble over territory and who delivers what escalating, and I'd say seeing the Mounties involved means it's escalated too far. You're an old friend, so I'm giving you the courtesy of letting you know," he paused and finished firmly, "I'm going to take care of this. However you want it done, I'll do it."

Abe could see the devil in Jake's eyes. He looked away and out the window past Harry. His hand found his leg, and he squeezed it, though he felt nothing. His memory drifted through the sunbeam, and he saw Theodora's smiling face. He was holding her close, her angelic glow warming him–filling him with love. He missed her so dearly. Were she here, she would know what to do. She would know exactly what to say. She would take his face in her hands and kiss his forehead, and whisper words of love and encouragement. His breath caught in his throat. If she were here, he wouldn't be laying in a bed with no feeling below his waist. He would be dancing with her in the snow.

After a moment of silent contemplation, Abe sniffed. "Run him out of town.

"I'd be willing to do more," Jake said plainly.

Abe looked at Harry. He wanted to give Jake his blessing, but he couldn't bring himself to do it. He was not a violent man. Never had been. "That just ain't the kind of man I am. I'm a bootlegger. Not a gangster."

Jake accepted that with a hint of resignation in his face. He rose from his chair. "Okay," he said and shook his friend's hand. He buttoned his coat and said, "I'll take care of it." He set the chair back against the wall and stepped to the door.

"My best to Rose," Abe said.

Harry stood flabbergasted. "What?" His words stopped Jake's exit. "Dad, Bradshaw doesn't deserve your mercy. If ever there was a reason to sink to the level of your enemy, it's now. It's unjust to treat him any other way."

Abe said gently, "This isn't the war, Hare."

"Yes, it is," he replied coldly. He faced Jake. "I can shoot."

Abe was stunned. "Harry—"

"Whatever you're planning to do, I can help. Take me with you." Harry took off his glasses and pocketed them in the front of his shirt.

Jake looked the young man up and down and then to Abe. "Yu trust him?"

Abe's eyes were wide, searching his son's face. He could see the soldier again. Harry looked taller, stronger, meaner, and Abe didn't know how to feel, but he responded without hesitation, "No one I trust more in the world."

Jake looked at Abe. His friend's brow was furrowed. "We doing it then?"

Abe swallowed. He couldn't take his eyes off his son, but he nodded.

Jake looked one last time at Harry, seeing the determination on his face. The young man was ready for war. "Good. We're going hunting. I'll be in my car when you're ready," Jake said and exited the room.

The two Calloways looked at one another. Abe let out a long, slow breath. "What are you doing?" he asked his son.

Harry looked at his hands. Distantly, he heard the boom of mortar shells and the shouts of comrades in arms. The haunting memories of the War were never far from his thoughts. He closed his eyes and forced them back down. They were replaced by visions of his father, broken and bloody and the cruel face of Fergus Bradshaw grinning like the devil himself.

Harry's voice was low, nearly a whisper, but firm. "I didn't fight the war I fought to see evil men tear the world apart."

"That was fighting for your country," Abe said.

Harry opened his eyes and found Abe's face. "And this is fighting for family. Nothing more important than that."

Father and son stared at one another from across the room, though it could have been miles. Each was struggling with their own demons, but both knew there was nothing either could do to change the other's mind. Abe inclined his head giving a silent blessing. Harry gave a small, curt nod and walked after Jake without another word.

Abe looked at the shaft of sunlight. He wished Theodora was here.

The passenger door to Jake's car slammed shut as Harry took a seat beside the old warrior. Jake peered at the younger man. He started the engine, threw the car in gear, and accelerated away from the hospital. The thin layer of snow crunched below the wheels. "Your dad's a strong son of bitch," he said.

"You've known him a long time?"

"Yep. The Finest moonshiner I've ever known."

Harry looked out the window, sadly. "It's the only thing he's ever been good at. I hope he'll get a chance to do it again."

"Do you now?" Jake said without looking away from the road. "Got the sense you aren't an ardent supporter of his criminal lifestyle."

Harry sat a moment, the car rocked back and forth as they rumbled along the coast. He thought about his father and the look on his face when he worked on his still. He thought of the glow that shone from the old man's face when he received compliments for his work. And he thought of the sadness in his tired eyes when a song would come on and Harry knew his father's heart was drifting back to his long departed wife. Harry said softly, "It makes him happy. Who am I to deny a man the thing that brings him joy?" He added with a dark tone filling his words, "And that bastard tried to take that from him."

Jake gazed at Harry. "This is more than that. You got revenge in your eyes, boy. You're looking to set something right, ain'tcha? Something in your being you looking to set proper."

Harry stared out his window. "I can't think about that right now."

"You can. You should. We're going to kill the man who put your dad in that hospital and that takes rage from the heart," Jake said and tapped a finger on his chest.

Harry sat in silence.

"Use it," Jake continued. "Use whatever hate you got in you, whether it's hate for these sons of bitches or something else. Only way to get it out is to let it out."

Harry drew a breath and nodded, more to himself than the old man's words.

CHAPTER TWENTY ONE

Tucked just off the main road of the island and through a thick pine treeline, an opulent Antebellum style mansion stood surrounded by forest. A long drive the length of a football field was lined with small pine trees and marble fixtures. The large box-like home was out of place on the Canadian island; the large pillars and balcony that ran along the entire outside edge of the house, evenly spaced large windows, and the big center entrance at the front and rear were far more typically found in the American South. A large barn was set in the back acres, the still hidden within. Several of Bradshaw's men, including RJ, milled about the porch and near the barn bundled in winter coats and hats. All of them armed with rifles and pistols. Some men smoked to stay warm. Earl Martin sat cleaning his rifle with his bandaged leg propped up on an apple box.

Though the winter sun shone brightly, dark clouds approached from the distance, slowly crawling across the horizon like a beast dragging itself nearer. The pristine, white Antebellum mansion shone in the light ready for the coming storm.

Jake's car appeared through the trees and pulled to a stop at the end of the drive about 100 meters away. RJ squinted at it and he rapped his knuckles on the barndoor. "Hey, boss! You expecting someone?"

Bradshaw stepped out of the barn in a stained apron and wiped his hands on a cloth. He scowled at the vehicle. "No, I'm not." Jake and Harry emerged from the car both holding rifles, and Bradshaw's face went white seeing Jake. "Shit," he said.

RJ looked to Bradshaw. The other men all sensed their boss' tension. Bradshaw yanked off his apron and shouted, "The hell you want, Jake Edwards?"

From the car, the old man shouted in return, "Boss Rose ain't happy with you, Fergus!"

"And why's that?" Bradshaw replied.

"You're starting fights with fellow bootleggers."

"A man has a right to claim his territory," Bradshaw smirked.

"This ain't your territory, boy. This is Boss Rose's island. You all just work for her."

"Well, maybe I'm looking to change that."

Jake and Harry stood on either side of the car. Bradshaw sneered. Earl rose from his chair and shouldered his rifle cockily. He grinned seeing Harry there.

"Hey, boy," Earl shouted. "How's your old man? I heard he survived. Next time I see him, I'll be sure to shoot him in the head and be done with him!"

Harry snapped his rifle up and fired a single bullet directly between Earl's eyes from 100 meters.

Bradshaw pointed sharply while shouting and sprinting to the house, "Take them out!"

The shout hit Jake's ears, and he reacted in a flash. As Bradshaw's men opened fire fast, Jake was faster. He fired his rifle like a gunslinger taking three out with three shots in a heartbeat.

Harry shouldered his rifle as well and killed two more. Bradshaw was just reaching the front door, and Harry turned his aim at him, chopping the wood with two shots but missing the gangster. Fergus turned on his heels and sprinted along the side of the house for the woods.

The gunfire came loud and sloppy from Bradshaw's men. Jake and Harry moved in tandem taking cover behind the pines and marble fixtures lining the drive. They picked off man after man, but more kept appearing. Bradshaw had collected a small army.

RJ reloaded behind a rusty wagon and hollered, "Come on! It's just some old man and a gimp!"

BAM! A bullet slammed against RJ's shoulder, and he spun to the dirt. He lost his gun in the fall and scrambled to reach it. Before he could, a shot from Jake found its mark in RJ's back, killing him.

Jake reloaded in a flash and shouted over the gunfire to Harry, "I got this! Go after Fergus! The woods!"

Harry, his limp barely noticeable, turned and raced toward the woods.

The dark clouds were over the estate now, and the snow finally came.

The flakes fell in clumps, and the world became a sheet of white. Bradshaw scrambled through the forest gasping for breath. The gunfire had ceased, but he had no way of knowing if that meant RJ and his men had won the day or if he was still in danger. So, he ran. He didn't know these woods. This had been his father's land. He had only moved here after the old bastard had died. He hadn't felt the need to stomp through the trees when he had a perfectly good mansion where he could spend his leisure time. His father had been the outdoorsy type. Fergus had always preferred the warmth of a fireplace and a comfy bed over deer hunting and animal snares, and perhaps, had he ever made an effort to indulge his father in his hobbies beyond making moonshine, Bradshaw would have known how to spot an animal trap before his foot landed in one.

Whoosh! The snare whipped out and caught him by the leg. It took him down in an instant. He roared in pain as the wire sliced through his pant leg and sliced into his skin. He pulled out a small knife and desperately began to cut the bloody wire.

BLAM! A shot smashed into the tree just next to Bradshaw causing him to shriek. He fired a look through the falling snow and could just make out two shadows approaching quickly. The men were closing in. Hands shaking, Bradshaw cut himself free and started to climb to his one good foot, but it was too late.

Another shot was fired into the air only meters away, and someone shouted from behind him, "That's far enough!"

Bradshaw froze. Breath coming in gasps, he swallowed the pain and attempted to maintain his composure. He raised his hands over his head remaining silent. The warm end of a rifle pressed into his back, and Bradshaw's heart skipped. Without turning around, he spit, "I knew you had the devil in you, boy. We know our own. You don't survive war without being a killer."

Harry stood directly behind Bradshaw seething. "I'm nothing like you, you son of a bitch."

"Well, you ain't like your pop!" Bradshaw shouted. "He's weak! Pathetic!"

Harry's boot found the back of Bradshaw's leg sending him to his knees grunting in pain.

"No, I'm not like him. He wanted you to live. Just wanted you run out of town."

Bradshaw spit blood and grinned with red teeth. "Heh. I wouldn't do the same. I'd see that old bastard dead and out of my territory."

Harry pressed the tip of his gun hard in Bradshaw's back. He desperately wanted to shoot the man, but something held him back. "Stop talking," he hissed.

Laughing, Bradshaw looked over his shoulder at Harry. "You won't get away with this. There'll be others. You think I'm the only one who knows this island is prime real estate for bootlegging? You kill me, someone else will take my place."

"Then I'll kill them too," Harry said darkly.

Bradshaw narrowed his eyes and lowered his hands a fraction of an inch. Harry had not shot him yet, and he could sense his hesitation. Slowly, Bradshaw turned and faced Harry. The snow fell around them thickly, enveloping the world in white.

Somewhere deep in Harry, the ghosts of his past were clawing at him begging to be released, while the hopes of a better life struggled to become tangible. His dreams of a simple life were as faded as the trees had become in the snow. He could hear his father's laugh and see his mother's perfect face. He could see his friends laughing drunkenly in London and feel the booms of war rattling his teeth. He saw the life he had as a child with love and kindness with his beautiful parents. He felt the sorrow of his father after his mother passed, and he felt the pull of war when he did not know what to do with the anger he felt with the world at taking her away. His heart thumped hard in his chest, and his fingers gripped the rifle in his hands. He would never find a perfect life. He would never have what he had as a child. He had only what the world had molded him into. He was a soldier, and he would always need a war to fight. In war, he knew who he was. In war, he could put his anger somewhere–his hate. And he had to put his hate somewhere.

He looked up in a daze and stared into the horrible face of Fergus Bradshaw towering over him, that cocky, sinister grin on his face. Harry lifted his gun, but his hands were shaking.

"You know how to soldier, boy. But you don't know what it takes to live this life," Bradshaw said. His hand darted out and slapped the end of the rifle away. Harry's finger squeezed the trigger, but the shot went wild. Bradshaw tackled Harry, and the two men fell to the snowy ground where they began to wrestle.

Bradshaw punched Harry in the side of the head. Harry put a knee swiftly into Bradshaw's stomach. Bradshaw wrapped his arm around Harry's neck and cranked him around. Harry grabbed Bradshaw by the ears and pulled. They both grunted and screamed in anger. They were like animals.

"Fuck!" Bradshaw shouted and hammered both fists directly into Harry's bum leg.

"GAH!" Harry screamed in agony, but he would not relent. He was a warrior, and he unleashed all of his anger, all of his frustration, all of his pain into the gangster. Fist after fist connected with Bradshaw's face until the man fell.

Bradshaw lay on his back coughing and bleeding profusely from the face. He groaned and rolled to his side. "You… I'll kill you… and your pop," he moaned. "I'll kill ya both, and I'll kill Jake Edwards and Rose…" he went on, but his mouth was so full of blood, Harry couldn't make out the words.

Harry stumbled to his feet and stood wobbling. He bent down and picked up his rifle. He pointed it at the moonshiner. Bradshaw looked up at him and spit a bloody tooth as Harry's feet. "See you hell—"

Harry pulled the trigger.

Blood splattered in the snow.

Fergus Bradshaw didn't have a chance to utter his last words.

The land was white with snow. Sunset had begun, the glow of the horizon pushing through the heavy snow clouds, as Harry wiped the dirt from his forehead and emerged from the trees, limping once again, worse now because of the fight. He found Jake walking through his handiwork. Dead and wounded men lay all over Bradshaw's land. Jake was entirely unharmed.

Harry reached him. "It's over," he said.

Jake nodded and asked no questions. He and Harry walked down the drive and back to the car.

CHAPTER TWENTY TWO

The snow had continued, the blanket of white muting the world. As the last light of the day was diminishing, Jake's car pulled up to Abe's shack. Harry exited the car and stood in the open door a moment. "Thank you," he said to the old man.

Jake nodded in stoic reply. He reached down and pulled out an envelope. He reached over the carseat and handed it to Harry. "For your Dad. From Rose."

Harry took it, offered a final farewell, and shut the door. Jake turned his car around and drove away. Harry pocketed the envelope and walked to the shack.

It was warm inside. A fire crackled in the stove. Harry had left it burning all day for Chip who, bandaged but otherwise well, limped from the bed to greet Harry. Harry bent and let the dog lick his face. He scratched the pup behind the ears and rose. Taking a lantern off the wall, Harry walked out the back door.

The thick canopy of evergreen trees had kept most of the snow away from the back of the shack. Harry walked the path to the still, which had a large tarp over it to protect it from the snowfall as well. He stood staring at the contraption for a moment. He ran his hand over it, respectfully. He bent down and started the machine. It chugged and spurted and then calmed, almost humming in the night.

Harry stood a long while just watching it work. He picked up an oil can and approached the still.

As the snow fell through the window, "The Nutcracker" twinkled through the radio in the corner of Abe's room at the hospital. Harry sat beside the bed and gently touched Abe's shoulder, and the old man woke with a start, grabbing Harry's arm instinctively.

"It's okay" Harry said quietly. "It's just me."

Abe breathed a sigh of relief, and then it dawned on him that Harry had returned and where he had been. "Bradshaw. Is he...?"

Harry nodded. "It's done."

"Where's Jake?"

"He left. Said he'd take care of the farm, whatever that means."

Abe nodded. He knew what it meant. There wouldn't be any mess to clean up with Fergus. He sighed and looked at his son. There was something different about the boy. A weight has been lifted from the boy's heart. "Are you okay?"

"I am," Harry said.

They sat in comfortable silence with one another. "Dance of the Sugar Plum Fairy" was just beginning, and the pair listened peacefully.

After a long while, Abe gave his leg a slap. "Well, now the big question - where do we go from here? Can't walk. Can't moonshine. Guess you got your Christmas wish. My booze-making days are behind me."

Harry put a hand on Abe's arm and smiled softly. "Not if you had an assistant."

Abe cocked an eyebrow at his son. He took his pinky finger and stuck is comically in his ear. "I'm sorry, I think you might have to repeat that. You pulling my leg? 'Cause that would be right nasty of you, boy."

Harry smiled and shrugged. "Already have a batch going. Started it this morning."

Abe laughed and blinked hard at this change of heart. "Unbelievable," he chuckled.

"I nearly lost you, Dad," Harry said.

"Life's short, Hare. I'm going to go some day. I've made peace with that. More or less, anyway."

Harry continued, "You're good at what you do, from what everyone tells me. But you're not going to be around forever."

"Not that I won't try," Abe winked.

Harry laughed. "The point is, you've built an incredible life for yourself, and I'm ready to be part of it. We've only got each other. We need to stick together."

Abe wiped an unbidden tear from his eye. "I've been waiting for a very long time to hear that from you, son."

"I'm just sorry it took me so long to figure it out," Harry said.

With nothing more to say, the two men hugged.

CHAPTER TWENTY THREE

Boss Rose O'Chauncey stood at her office window looking uncharacteristically nervous. The waves of the bay were rough today, tipped with foamy white, and the snow had fallen just as much here in Portland as it had on Texada. She had a fire going in the corner fireplace, but she still rubbed her hands together for warmth.

The door to the room opened, and Jake entered. She turned to face him.

"Fergus is gonna be a bit short on his last shipment," Jake reported.

Rose's face did not betray any emotion. "Oh?" was all she offered.

"I used it to burn down his house."

"I see you decided to handle things with force," Rose said and moved to a small drink cart against the wall where she poured herself a glass of brown liquid.

"He shot Abe in the guts," Jake said.

Rose froze, her back to her enforcer. Her heartbeat skipped, but she was able to keep her voice level. "Is he alive?"

"Calloway's too pigheaded to die," Jake replied. "He's well enough. His legs aren't working proper, but I gave him and his boy enough to pay every doctor from here to New York City. He'll work something out."

Rose relaxed and finished pouring her drink. She took a sip and paced a bit. She stopped and touched a framed photograph on her desk. A young Abe stood beside a young Rose. She touched his face with her fingertip and asked with quiet concern "Do you think he'll be alright?"

Jake respectfully answered as though he had not heard the care in the woman's voice, "That stubborn old coot always has something up his sleeve, Boss."

Rose smiled to herself, her affection for Abe Calloway clearly in her heart. She allowed the moment to linger, and then she cleared her throat and changed her entire demeanor. "Very well," she said and strolled to the window. "We'll need to make arrangements to fill the hole left by Bradshaw. Rumor has it Canada is ending this little prohibition experiment by the end of the year, while things are only getting more heated in Washington over all this. Good for us," she added with a grin. "We won't have to worry about any of our Northern friends getting pinched by Mounties." She raised her glass to her lips and paused, lowering it and turning to face Jake. "You know, Jake, I'm thinking it's time we expanded our budding empire." Her smile widened, and she turned back to the window.

She looked out at the waves and squinted as her calculating mind churned with pleasurable thoughts.

Marshall rowed out of the darkness, as he approached the shore. He waved his lantern at the figure standing on the dock with the dog beside him. Marshall went to greet his old friend but stopped short with amused shock.

Harry was standing there with Chip.

Marshall landed the boat and hopped out onto the snowy bank. "I wasn't sure you'd show," he said. "Good to see you, Harry." The two men shook hands. Chip barked. "You too, boy," Marshall laughed.

"Dad said you were a good teacher," Harry said.

Marshall chuckled, "Did he now? Well, at smuggling, yeah, if that what you wanna learn."

Harry rubbed his gloved hands together and rocked on the balls of his feet. "That's where he suggested I start with while he recovers. And I figured it wouldn't hurt having an extra set of eyes and a rifle on board."

Marshall smiled broadly. "I like the sound of that." He glanced at his boat. He had patched up the bullet holes, but the old craft still looked worse for wear.

"Thanks, Marhall," Harry said.

"Haven't done nothing yet," he replied.

"I mean, thanks for always being there for my Dad. You're a good man."

Marshall shrugged off the compliment. He was not used to receiving praise. "Come on, let's load up."

The two men carried a few barrels and a half dozen crates of mason jars into the rowboat. Harry hopped on board with Chip, and they shoved off.

Marshall took the oars and spoke as he rowed, "We got a big pick up at Secret Cove and another at Egmont. We're going to be busy all night moving that much stuff. Hopefully the temperature don't drop too much." He leaned closer to Harry adding coyly, "Then again, that just means we can warm up on some of your dad's samples." He wagged his eyebrows and laughed heartily.

Harry smirked at the man, and the two bootleggers drifted into the winter night.

CHAPTER TWENTY FOUR

25 December 1920

The sun dazzled over the snowy swamplands of Texada Island painting the Canadian landscape in a porcelain-white glow, speckling the frosty pine trees and rippling over the frozen, crystal waters. It was peaceful, a serene Christmas Day in the undisturbed wilderness. The steady rhythm of the breeze on the barren trees and soft pitter patter of critters scampering through the snow was broken by the sound of heavy footfalls down the path to Abe's shack.

Harry walked with a catch of fresh salmon slung over his shoulder. He pounded his boots clear of snow and mud on the porch and walked into the cabin.

Inside, the warm fire glowed in the stove, and the decorated Christmas tree jangled in the corner; Chip was underneath it sniffing around the wrapped gifts. Candles were set in the window, and other decorations were hanging on the walls and shelves. It was festive and quaint. Abe sat in his wheelchair in a clean, newly knit jumper from Bessie. He'd received it by courier the day before with a note that stated simply: *Merry Christmas – Bess*. It was the nicest thing she'd ever said, Abe joked.

Marshall stood in the kitchen drinking a hot cocoa. He had attempted to comb his hair back with some sort of pomade. The top was flat while the back stuck out at odd points. He had done his best.

"How are you liking the chair?" Harry smiled.

Abe gave the wheels a push and coasted around the small cabin. "It feels great!"

"Good," Harry beamed. "Merry Christmas, Dad." Harry gave Abe a quick hug.

"I'll take those," Marshall said. He shook Harry's hand as he took the collection of fish.

Abe deftly rolled to the kitchen area and bumped into the table. He reached up and clasped the mason jar set beside three glasses. He poured the amber liquid into the glasses. "Boys, I'd like to propose a toast." Harry and Marshall accepted their glasses from the old man. "A toast to new beginnings and a passing of the torch."

Marshall raised his glass and added, "And to generous compensation."

"And to Boss Rose and her mighty empire," Abe said.

"And to all the thirsty drinkers out there," Harry chimed in and raised his glass too.

Abe laughed. "Cheers, gentlemen."

They clinked their glasses and Abe slung his shot down easily, and Marshall flinched slightly at the burn of the alcohol.

They looked at Harry expectantly. Harry smirked, raised his shoulders, and let them drop before saying, "Down the hatch." He tilted his head back and poured the shot down his throat. His eyes went wide and his voice cracked hoarsely, "Oh sweet Lord."

The elder men laughed loudly at Harry's expense. Even Chip barked happily.

Abe rolled to the radio and flicked it on just as "Winter Wonderland" by Lew Stone came on, and the men continued to drink and laugh. Harry took a seat and took very careful sips of his drink. Marshall played with Chip, now healed and yipping around happily.

Harry patted Abe's shoulder gladly. "Whenever you're ready to come back, I'd love to learn more about your process."

"From what Marshall tells me, you're already on your way to mastering the chemistry of it all."

Harry shook his head humbly. "We just follow your recipe, and he keeps an eye on me. So far, we've done alright." Harry suppressed a teasing smile and added, "Maybe you could even take a few more weeks off?"

Abe laughed loudly. "You'd like, eh!"

Harry laughed along with him. "I love ya, Dad. And I'm ready to learn everything you can teach me."

"Patience, my boy. All in good time," Abe smiled and beamed at his son. This all meant more to him than Harry might ever realize.

Weeks passed, and the new year began with more snow and the repeal of Prohibition in British Columbia, but the nationwide ban of alcohol in America continued for the years to come. Boss Rose had pushed all her Northern bootleggers to work twice as hard to meet the booming demand for booze, and the Calloways were more than happy to oblige.

Marshall and Harry loaded the boat on the docks of Texada on the Strait of Georgia. No more hiding in the swamps.

Harry was more anxious than usual. "Now, you'll be extra careful with this batch, won't you?"

Marshall chuckled, "Give it a rest, boy. I know what I'm doing."

"It's my first true batch," Harry said. "I'm just—"

"As nervous as a mama seeing her babe off to their first day of school. Yeah, yeah," Marshall rolled his eyes.

From beside the truck, Abe sat in his chair with a thick blanket wrapped around his legs. He watched Marshall and Harry put the rowboat into the water. He patted Chip on the head. "Doesn't get any better, Chip. I got my boy back and I still got you." He smiled, though a gentle longing came over his expression. He looked up at the sky. A break in the clouds showed the sun, and Abe felt the warmth on his cheeks. He closed his eyes for a moment and felt Theodora's hands on his face–her soft lips on his. "Well," he said quietly, "I suppose it could be a little better."

"Dad!" Harry called from the water. "We'll see you in two days."

"Smooth sailing," Abe said with a wave.

"You sure you're alright getting back?" Marshall shouted.

"I'll be fine," Abe waved a dismissive hand.

Marshall and Harry pushed the boat out together, and they drifted off toward the ocean waters. Harry looked back and waved to Abe. Marshall rowed them away. Abe waved to him and sat a long while on the beach until the row boat was long gone.

He braced himself with both hands on the arms of his chair and attempted to stand. He struggled a moment and then plopped back down. He tried again, this time he rose from his chair, planted his feet, and stood fully. He grabbed his cane. Carefully, he took a step on the rocky beach, and then another. Chip watched him with care. Abe struggled on his feet but eventually found his stride. Once he stopped wobbling, he walked slowly down the beach with Chip. He took in the warm sun and didn't mind the cold breeze across his cheeks. He looked out at the fishing boats and then off to the hills. The tops of the buildings and homes of Texada were easy to see through the sparse trees. As his eyes traced a trail of smoke from a chimney, he considered making a visit to Bessie. He smiled to himself wondering if they'd manage to have a decent conversation before he annoyed her.

The sun shone brilliantly, glistening off the waves, and Abe strolled along the water's edge, content.

THE END